Dancing Queen

D0734043

How Not to Spend Your Senior Year
BY CAMERON DOKEY

Royally Jacked
BY NIKI BURNHAM

Ripped at the Seams
BY NANCY KRULIK

Spin Control
BY NIKI BURNHAM

Cupidity
BY CAROLINE GOODE

South Beach Sizzle
BY SUZANNE WEYN AND DIANA GONZALEZ

She's Got the Beat
BY NANCY KRULIK

30 Guys in 30 Days
BY MICOL OSTOW

Animal Attraction
BY JAMIE PONTI

A Novel Idea
BY AIMEE FRIEDMAN

Scary Beautiful
BY NIKI BURNHAM

Getting to Third Date
BY KELLY McCLYMER

Dancing Queen

ERIN DOWNING

Simon Pulse
New York London Toronto Sydney

This book is a work of fiction. Any references to historical events, real people, or real locales are used fictitiously. Other names, characters, places, and incidents are the product of the author's imagination, and any resemblance to actual events or locales or persons, living or dead, is entirely coincidental.

SIMON PULSE
An imprint of Simon & Schuster
Children's Publishing Division
1230 Avenue of the Americas
New York, NY 10020
Copyright © 2006 by Erin Soderberg Downing
All rights reserved, including the right of reproduction in whole or in part in any form.
SIMON PULSE and colophon are registered trademarks of Simon & Schuster, Inc.
Designed by Ann Zeak
The text of this book was set in Garamond 3.
Manufactured in the United States of America
First Simon Pulse edition June 2006
10 9 8 7 6 5 4 3 2
Library of Congress Control Number 2006920561
ISBN-13: 978-1-4169-2510-1
ISBN-10: 1-4169-2510-4

For Milla, my little rock star
and for Greg, who rocks

Acknowledgments

Huge thanks to my fabulously fun editor and friend, Michelle Nagler, as well as the amazing Bethany Buck and the rest of the crew at Simon Pulse for taking a chance on me with this book.

This book wouldn't have been possible without my husband, Greg, who makes me laugh and appreciates my quirks.

Many hugs (hee hee!) to Robin Wasserman, my writing buddy extraordinaire.

And cheers to my incredible mom, who eagerly read and praised every draft of this book (even the really bad first round); my dad, who is just supercool and who forgave me for not using my maiden name (Soderberg) on the cover of this book; Sarah, who has been a superstar friend for twenty years and who made that first trip to London phenomenal; and Josef, Anna, Anders, and Stockholm—for helping to bring this book to life in Sweden and introducing me to the Eurovision Song Contest.

Also, hooray for ABBA, whose music makes me happy!

Dancing Queen

Super Freak

Olivia Phillips's first-ever celebrity sighting was going all wrong.

She had just landed flat on her butt, her long legs splayed at awkward angles across a busy sidewalk in the middle of central London. She had a discarded cigarette butt stuck to her jeans, her face was splotchy, and her curly brown hair was stuck to her lip gloss. Though she didn't want to look, she was pretty sure the bottom of one leg of her jeans had crept up above the cuff of her athletic sock and gotten stuck there.

Liv—as her friends called her—couldn't remember a time in recent history she had looked *less* fabulous.

Tragically, it was at this very moment that

Josh Cameron, International Pop Star and *Celeb* magazine's Hottest Guy of 2006, was staring straight at her. *The* Josh Cameron, whom Liv had fantasized about a million and three times, was standing less than two feet away, casting a shadow from his perfect body onto Liv's disheveled figure on the sidewalk.

Why, Liv wondered, *do things like this always happen to me?* She had arrived in London from Ann Arbor, Michigan, less than two hours earlier . . . and she had already made a complete fool of herself in front of the world's biggest celebrity. *How is this even possible?!*

Because Liv was Liv. And she had a tendency to turn ordinary embarrassing moments into extraordinarily embarrassing ones—which meant this moment could get a whole lot worse. And it did.

Looking up at Josh Cameron, Liv was unable to stop a goofy, uncomfortable sort of smile from spreading across her face. She lifted her hand in a little wave and—very much against her will—blurted out, "Cheerio!"

Three hours earlier . . .

Gazing out the airplane window at London's sprawling suburbs miles below her, Liv couldn't believe she was actually here. In her sleep-deprived state, it *still* didn't feel real that she had been selected as one of Music Mix Europe's summer interns. But now that she was settled into a cramped window seat and minutes away from landing on the other side of the Atlantic, she finally let it sink in: She would be living in London!

Liv had spent every waking minute since she had gotten her acceptance letter daydreaming about days surrounded by rock stars and nights out tra-la-la-ing from club to club. Of course, deep down, she knew the Music Mix internship would be a lot of work, too. But she had somehow managed to avoid thinking about that part. Why not focus on the good stuff?

When the plane landed, Liv grabbed her black wheelie from baggage claim and followed airport signs to the Gatwick Express. Hustling through the terminal with her suitcase and overstuffed carry-on tote, Liv's excitement bubbled into giddiness. She heaved her stuff onto the train into the city, and a chirpy English voice wished her a good day and a pleasant journey. She just loved the British accent. It always sounded so civilized and kind.

The train began to roll toward downtown London as Liv flipped through the on-board magazine, reading about London's neighborhoods. Music Mix was setting her up with an apartment as part of the internship—she couldn't wait to find out where her roommates would be from, and where they would be living. Notting Hill, Chelsea, Greenwich . . . they all sounded fantastic.

Since she had never been anywhere more exotic than Ely, Minnesota, they all sounded a little intimidating and foreign, too. She had only lived away from home once before (Liv always gagged when she thought about that terrible summer her dad had decided to send her to an all-girls camp on Lake Michigan), so this was definitely going to be an adventure.

Paging through the magazine, Liv quickly studied British lingo and discovered that if she wanted to fit in, her roommates would actually be flatmates, the subway is the tube, and she absolutely must eat something called bangers and mash.

Eventually the train heaved out one final puff, and the doors sighed open to let Liv out into central London. She had arrived!

Making her way into Victoria train station, Liv scanned the signs overhead, looking for the London Underground. Dodging through the crowd, she found an open ticket booth and bought a monthly travel card. Studying the tube map in her guidebook, Liv found the route to Oxford Street, home of Music Mix Europe's central office. She had been told to "pop by" the studio to pick up keys to her flat.

Hustling through the corridor toward the tube, Liv eyed the advertisements pasted on the walls. Next to an ad for Cadbury chocolates (*Yum . . . must get some of that*), Liv spotted a poster of Josh Cameron. She slowed her walk slightly, scanning the advertisement for details.

JOSH CAMERON: SPECIAL APPEARANCE, LIVE IN LONDON! Liv stopped briefly—her eye had been drawn to a small detail in the lower corner of the ad: "Sponsored by Music Mix Europe." Liv wondered if she would get to help with the concert. . . . That certainly wouldn't be a bad way to spend the summer. She was just the tiniest bit obsessed with Josh Cameron, and would give pretty much anything to meet him in person. There weren't a lot of celebrities floating around Ann Arbor.

Liv could hear the subway train rolling

into the station just ahead of her, and she hustled to catch it. She pulled her suitcase and carry-on clear of the doors just before they swooshed closed and the train roared out of the station. Two stops later the train's doors slid open and she stepped onto the platform as a freakishly polite mechanical voice reminded her to "mind the gap." Liv •passed through one of the arches leading her away from the platform and rode the long escalator up and out onto the street. Red double-decker buses breezed past, stuffed with passengers out for a day of shopping. People packed the sidewalk, hustling past Liv, who stood rooted to her spot just outside the Underground exit.

The noise and speed of the crowd was overwhelming. The time difference had started to catch up with her, and Liv realized that it was the middle of the night back in Michigan. Hit with a wave of sleepiness, Liv glanced down Oxford Street and spotted the glowing Music Mix sign.

She applied a coat of gloss to her lips and hastily made her way toward the sign. She lifted her suitcase, slinging her carry-on tote over a shoulder, and pushed into the office's revolving entrance doors.

Liv's reflexes had slowed from lack of

sleep, and she realized too late that she had forgotten to get out of the revolving door on the inside and was back out on Oxford Street. Blushing, she made another turn around in the door and stepped out into the large, open lobby, tucking a stray curl behind her ear. She looked around quickly to make sure no one had seen her mistake. Coast clear.

Liv smiled widely as she approached the security desk. "Excuse me . . . I'm one of Music Mix's summer interns. Can you tell me where should I go?"

The security guard looked up briefly, then returned to the tabloid he was reading. "Third floor, miss." Liv muttered a quick thanks, resisting the urge to curtsy, and took the escalator up. She stepped into a round, colorful sitting area whose walls were filled with floor-to-ceiling television screens playing a variety of music videos.

As Liv approached the circular desk in the center of the room, she could hear the receptionist chatting animatedly. Peeking up over the edge of the tall desk, Liv could see that the receptionist's dyed blond hair was formed into a dozen long thick dreadlocks and was pulled back from her face with a hot pink scarf. She was wearing a short strapless dress and an armful of silver bangles that set off her dark skin perfectly. She motioned to Liv to wait, and quickly finished up her conversation.

Looking up at Liv, she smiled. "Welcome to Music Mix. Here to check in?"

Liv grinned. "Yes, I am. My name is Olivia Phillips."

"It's lovely to meet you, Olivia. I'm Gloria. Here's the scoop: I give you keys to your flat, and you're on your own for today. Settle in, meet your flatmates, get some sleep. Just be back here at nine tomorrow morning. Simon Brown can be a bit testy in the morning, so don't be late—it's best to stay on his good side."

Liv recalled that her acceptance letter had come from a guy named Simon Brown—she now realized he must be the one in charge. What a fabulous job.

Gloria shuffled through a box on her desk and plucked out a small yellow envelope. She pulled out two keys and a card with an address printed on it. Scanning the card, Gloria passed it across the desk to Liv, along with the keys. She pulled a pocket-size London Underground map out of her desk drawer and circled one of the stops in hot pink marker.

"You're sharing a flat with two other girls," Gloria explained. "They have both checked in with me already, so they should be at the flat when you get there. Think you can find it?"

Liv nodded again and turned toward the escalator. "Thanks a lot. I'll see you tomorrow." Gloria smiled and pushed a button to answer the phone that had just started ringing.

Riding the escalator down, Liv could see that the Music Mix lobby had become much more crowded since she had arrived just a few minutes earlier. She scanned the faces and chic outfits as she passed, wishing she were dressed just a little cuter and didn't have her bulky wheelie and carry-on—she *knew* she looked like a tourist.

Liv glanced down to study the tube map as she made her way into the revolving door to leave the building. Distracted, she didn't notice someone step off Oxford Street and into the door as she exited.

Suddenly, Liv was jolted backward. As she lost her balance, both Liv and her wheelie toppled over onto the sidewalk. Though she had come out on the right side of the door this time, her bulky carry-on bag had not been so lucky. The strap of the bag was still attached securely to Liv's shoulder, but the bag itself was stuck on the other side of the glass in the compartment behind her. The revolving door had come to a complete standstill.

Liv pulled her arm out of the bag's strap to release it and craned her neck around, hoping no one was stuck in the door. Her face reddened as she realized that someone was definitely standing—trapped—in the other glass compartment. The person turned to face her, and Liv's mouth dropped open.

Staring at her from the other side of the glass, stuck in a revolving door between Oxford Street and the Music Mix lobby, was Josh Cameron.

Back to the future . . .

It felt like hours had gone by. Josh Cameron had quickly freed himself and Liv's bag from the door and was now standing—staring— at Liv on the ground. And was it her imagination, or had she just shouted "cheerio" to the world's biggest pop star? Liv straightened her legs, but continued to sit on the sidewalk, stumped and horrified. *Nice first impression, Liv. Suave.*

Josh Cameron smiled as he held Liv's

carry-on out to her. "I believe this is yours. . . ."

"Um, thanks." *Um, thanks? Really great response . . . very witty and charming.*

Josh Cameron tilted his head to the side just slightly and looked at Liv with concern. "Are you okay? That looked like a pretty bad fall." She scrambled to her feet and took her bag from him, groping for the right words.

Come on, supersexy girl within, Liv begged inwardly, *say something clever and alluring! Oh God, you're just staring. . . . Say* something*!* "Yeah, I'm fine. Just a little embarrassed. You don't think anyone saw that, do you? Hah hah hah!" Liv laughed too loudly at her own nonjoke, quickly straightening her hair and brushing the cigarette butt off her jeans.

"I'm Olivia, by the way. And I'm really sorry. It's just that, well, my friends always say this is the kind of thing that I do, uh, you know, when I guess I want to meet celebrities, or, um, make a winning first impression, or uh . . . hah hah hah," *Shut up, just SHUT UP! What are you talking about?!*

Josh Cameron was smiling at her, clearly amused. He patiently ran a hand through his gorgeous curls as Liv stuttered through her ridiculous monologue. By the time she finally had the self-control to shut up, he had begun to laugh.

"Well, Olivia, I better be off. It's been lovely meeting you. I really do hope you're not hurt." As he made his way back through the revolving door, Josh Cameron turned once more and looked at Liv. He smiled his famous smile, and walked into the lobby toward the waiting crowd.

Liv stared after him for a few seconds, then backed away from Music Mix's front doors. She was pleased to see that her white athletic sock was definitely poking up over the cuff of her jeans. *Really cute, Liv. Very chic.*

As her mind replayed the past five minutes over and over—coming up with about twelve significantly more glamorous ways she could have met the biggest pop star in the world—Liv made her way back to the tube and toward her new home. She had been in London less than three hours, and had already managed to fit in a lifetime's worth of humiliation. And, much as she hated to admit it, Liv suspected this wasn't the end of it.

She Drives Me Crazy

Emerging from the subway, Liv detected the faint odor of urine. She covered her nose and hurried out onto the sidewalk, turning left and heading toward the address listed on the card she had gotten from Gloria.

She couldn't help feeling a little concerned as she took in her surroundings. Liv's image of London had come from movies like *Bridget Jones's Diary* and *What a Girl Wants*. This wasn't quite the same. All the buildings looked shabby, and there were more fish and chips shops than people.

She stopped at a medium-size gray building at the end of the block. The iron gate led into a small flowerless courtyard, with three huge garbage cans resting at the foot of a set of stairs that led upward.

Liv double-checked the address on her card and pulled the keys from her pocket. The biggest key worked, and Liv made her way into the courtyard and toward the stairs. Hers was apartment 523. She looked for the elevator, but immediately realized she wouldn't find one. Climbing slowly with her suitcase, Liv got to the fifth floor sweaty and out of breath. She figured the walk up was a good thing—her butt would look fantastic by the end of the summer.

As she made her way down the hall, Liv's heart began to beat faster. She was about to meet her new flatmates. *Where will they be from?* She wondered. *Paris? Milan? New York?* Liv turned the key and pushed open the door.

She was greeted with three enormous, obscenely expensive-looking Armani suitcases. Each was propped open, displaying a treasure chest of Gucci and Zac Posen, a pile of cashmere, and several very real-looking alligator pumps. Caught off guard, Liv stood silently in the doorway for a few minutes before stumbling into the room and pushing her generic wheelie against a wall.

Breathing heavily from her climb, Liv glanced around the room. It wasn't exactly charming, but it would certainly do. The room was mostly naked of furniture, which was a pretty good thing considering that the three huge suitcases took up most of the floor space anyway. Directly across from the front door was a slim counter, which overlooked a tiny kitchen. There were three small bar stools squeezed under the countertop. Along the right wall was an ironing board, jammed in next to an antique-looking stereo.

Liv quickly scanned the rest of the room. Her eyes came to rest on a short threadbare couch along the wall. It looked like it might have been flowered once, but was now just a pale shade of green. Liv realized that there was a wisp of a girl perched delicately on one arm of the couch. The girl was looking Liv up and down without any hint of subtlety.

Liv bellowed out a very loud "hi there" to hide her surprise and discomfort at (1) realizing someone was sitting on the sofa looking at her, and (2) realizing that that someone was very obviously studying her for flaws.

After an awkward moment of silence, the girl introduced herself as Rebecca, a self-described "Texas Honey." Liv quickly stated her name in response, and then Rebecca released a delicate sigh and launched into a list of house rules, nearly all of which related to Rebecca's clothes and what Liv could and couldn't touch (the "Could" list was blank, as far as Liv could tell).

"And most important," Rebecca explained in her thick Texas drawl, "Ah am to be called Rebecca—that is Rah*beh*kaw. Not Becky or Becks or Becca or any other fun little nicknames you might devise. My father taught me that this manner of coziness is tacky." A quick hair flip, and then Rebecca lifted her tiny body off the couch and swayed down a hallway.

Liv had said nothing more than "hi there," and already she felt like a goon. *Just my luck,* Liv thought, watching Rebecca retreat down the hall. *I come all the way to London and get stuck with* that.

Luckily, Liv's other roommate (*flatmate,* she reminded herself) was good-ol'-Becky's polar opposite. Anna, a calm, gorgeous blonde from Sweden, appeared a few minutes after Rebecca had closed her glossy lips and swept away.

Anna introduced herself by confessing that she would have come out sooner to say hello, but she had been avoiding Rebecca since the two of them had arrived at the apartment a few hours earlier. "She promised to show me the photo album from her last beauty pageant," Anna said simply. "I just couldn't deal." Liv could already tell she was going to like Anna.

"So," Liv said, grabbing the handle of her wheelie. She was dying to get out of her jeans—she'd been in the same clothes ever since she left Michigan more than twenty-four hours before. "You guys probably already picked rooms, right? Which one is mine?"

A sweet, high-pitched voice came trilling down the hall. *Rebecca*, Liv cringed as the tiny blonde came swaying back into the living room. Rebecca smiled, visibly glowing as she said dramatically, "Li-uhv, *this* is your room."

Anna glanced around the living room. "I'm sorry, Liv. There are only two little bedrooms, and the couch pulls out. . . . I'm sure it won't be that bad."

Liv turned slowly, surveying the couch. "Right . . . ," she said. She sat down on the couch and felt her butt squish a full two feet through the fabric until it was resting only a few inches off the floor. "Great. Well then, I'm just going to get settled." She smiled weakly.

Anna studied Liv carefully before turning and heading down the hall to her room. She called out, "Let me know if you need anything, okay? I mean it . . . anything."

Rebecca just stood there, arms crossed, batting her cold eyes at Liv. "You're such a good sport, Li-uhv. Ah think you'll be so comfy out here." And then she winked—yes, winked—and trilled a high-pitched laugh as she skipped down the hallway toward her bedroom.

Liv hoisted herself out of the couch and pushed one of Rebecca's suitcases out of her way with her foot. She would have much rather jumped inside the suitcase and stomped on all the clothes, but she realized that probably wasn't the first impression she wanted to make. It wasn't *Rebecca's* fault she was stuck sleeping on a fold out couch. Though Rebecca *had* seemed to get an unnatural thrill from breaking the news.

As she pulled her wheelie out of the corner, Liv spotted a small British flag embroidered on the bottom corner of her suitcase. *Uh-oh,* she thought. She turned the suitcase over and lifted the flap that hid the nameplate. The name Millie Banks stared back at her.

Noooooooooooooo! Reality very quickly sank in: her bag, and with it all of her carefully chosen outfits, was gone. She must have taken the wrong suitcase from baggage claim, and now she was stuck with this one. It was identical to hers—except for the little flag.

The good news was that Millie Banks lived in London, and there was a phone number. Liv could only hope she and Millie had made an even swap so they could easily trade back and laugh about how funny this all was. Though at this moment Liv didn't find anything about the situation amusing.

She eagerly pulled the stranger's suitcase into the middle of the floor and tugged at the zipper—she figured it couldn't hurt to look. As it was, Liv had the jeans and T-shirt she had been wearing for two days, and that was it. She needed *something* to wear on her first day of work, and she quietly prayed that the suitcase would be stuffed with a fabulous selection of designer duds.

It wasn't.

Looking up at her from inside the stranger's black suitcase were seven little white dogs, each embroidered on a different color sweater. She unfolded the turquoise sweater with a dog-in-a-bonnet design and sighed.

As she sat staring at the half-dozen

doggies and wondering what to do next, Rebecca breezed into the living room. Little Miss Texas was going full-speed ahead on a one-sided conversation—Liv suspected that Rebecca enjoyed hearing herself talk, and didn't really care whether anyone was listening or responding.

"Oh, Li-uhv, those are just such cute little sweaters. One doggie sweater a day. Precious. Very chic." Rebecca tinkled out a laugh and swept a pile of Armani from the ironing board into her arms.

"Yeah, they're just adorable." Liv bit her lip and continued. "Rebecca, I don't suppose there's any chance you have anything in one of your suitcases that I could borrow for work tomorrow? I picked up the wrong suitcase at the airport, and as cute as these little collies are, I just don't think they'll cut it."

"Oh, Li-uhv." Rebecca sighed. "Those are *westies*, not collies. And no, I'm afraid I just don't have anything that will work on you—you're too big. Maybe Anna has something in your size?" She tilted her head and smiled. "Besides, Ah just don't think I have anything I can spare. I get oozy about people borrowing my clothes. Stains and such . . ."

"Great," Liv said sarcastically, ignoring Rebecca's jabs. "That's just great. I'll talk to Anna."

"About what?" Anna had just walked into the living room with an enormous apple. She plunked down into the couch, took a bite, and folded her legs up under herself.

"I was just asking Rebecca if I could borrow something to wear to work tomorrow, but she doesn't have anything she can spare." Liv cringed and held up the purple sweater with a dog-in-a-basket design. "I swapped bags with someone at the airport. I'm not sure this is going to go over well at Music Mix. Help?"

"Of course." Anna stood up quickly and headed to her bedroom. As she turned and beckoned Liv to follow, she briefly made a face in Rebecca's direction. "Let me show you what I have."

An hour later Liv and Anna finally stopped laughing long enough to pose for a photo next to the living statue in Leicester Square. When they had first approached the silver figure, Liv thought the statue was metal— but realized it was actually a live person after the mouth released a loud screech and the statue's joints shifted position.

Liv popped a ten-pence coin into the hat in the figure's outstretched silver hand, and jumped when the human-statue robotically shifted position to say thanks. Laughing again, she grabbed Anna's arm and moved toward the center of the square.

"I still can't believe Rebecca thought I was going to be excited about that velour thing." Liv and Anna had spent the whole tube ride from their apartment to central London dwelling on Rebecca's unwillingness to share her clothes. Liv was even more stumped by the fact that after her original no, Rebecca had apparently changed her mind and generously offered Liv a zip-up crushed velvet jogging suit, saying it was "all she could spare."

"I know! She spent the whole morning bragging to me about how she had packed three suitcases so she would be prepared for anything." Anna shook her head and giggled. "There must be *something* she can part with for a day."

"Well, let's celebrate the fact that we got out of the apartment tonight. I have no doubt we would have been stuck watching a fashion show if we had stuck around." Liv switched to a thick Southern drawl. "Ah mean, what on earth is she goin' ta wa-uhr ta-mah-row?"

Anna laughed, and suddenly Liv felt a little bad about making fun of Rebecca. But on second thought, Liv had gotten no signs of kindness from her at all. And life was too short to bother with people who were going to treat her like a second-class citizen. She was just lucky she had Anna to laugh it off with.

They settled onto an empty bench in the center of Leicester Square. Anna had arranged to meet up with two Music Mix interns she had met that morning when she was checking in, and had invited Liv to tag along.

As they sat and waited, Liv leaned back into the bench and gazed around at the pigeons and camera-happy tourists who filled the square. Breathing in the damp London air, Liv couldn't help but think about her mom, Isobel, who had grown up in London. Though her mom had died more than ten years earlier, Liv could still hear her voice—with its lovely, lilting English accent—saying that London was the best place on earth.

What was it that made her believe that? Liv wondered. *Did she ever sit in this square with her friends, looking at the same buildings I am now, when she was a teenager?* After her mother died, Liv had sworn to her father that she would live in London someday. She intended to find out what her mother's life had been like and what had made her love England so much, even years after she had moved away.

"How did you convince your parents to let you come to London?" Anna asked, pulling Liv out of her memories.

"Well, my mom died a long time ago, so it's just me and my dad," Liv explained. "My dad is a photographer, so it helped to play up the whole developing-my-inner-artist thing. And I don't think it hurt that he was offered a gig doing a photo shoot for some rich Italian businessman this summer—he gets to spend the summer on Lake Como in Italy. He seemed to like the idea that we'd be on the same continent. It all just worked out, I guess."

"You're lucky—it sounds like he was pretty cool about it," Anna said, lowering her eyes. "I had the hardest time getting my parents to let me come. My mom is certain I'll be a doctor, and this is about as far from med school as you can get. She told me I could have this summer to 'play,' as she calls it, but I had to promise to re-evaluate my priorities when I get back to Sweden." Anna sighed. "I just wish she would back off some. I mean, I'm nineteen. I should be making my own decisions." Anna shrugged and smiled weakly.

"You're nineteen?" Liv couldn't believe it—Anna was two years older than her, and already out of high school. "Actually, I guess I'm surprised that my dad let me come at all. But he moved out on his own when he was sixteen to take pictures of rock stars and 'live the seventies life.'" Liv made little quotation marks in the air. "I think he feels like he owes it to his childhood self to trust me."

"Wow. Your dad sounds fabulous. The complete opposite of my parents."

"Remember, this is all in theory." Liv smiled, picturing her dad struggling to mix his liberal ideals with his idea of what a good dad should be like. "In reality, he's pretty strict. But we have a lot of fun together." Liv smiled, suddenly missing her dad. "What do you want to do, if you're not into med school?" Liv asked Anna, wishing she had even the slightest idea of what she wanted to do when she graduated from high school next year. She had tried to avoid thinking about it, but realized decision-time was coming way too soon.

"I'm not sure," Anna said, frustrated. "Honestly, I've been dying to work at Music Mix for ages. That's really all I've ever wanted. If this summer goes the way I hope, I'll get a job offer at the end—which I'm sure will devastate my mom." Anna sighed and looked around the square before continuing. "But it's not going to happen, so there's no point in getting my hopes up. I just know I don't want to go to med school—yet. I guess I need some time before I'm forced to figure my life out."

"Does your mom know that?" Liv asked, noticing how upset Anna had gotten while talking about her future.

Anna shook her head. "I've already been accepted into a few great schools for next year, so Mom's taken it as a sign that I'm supposed to go right on to university. Unless something major happens this summer, I'll be at Oxford or Stockholm University in the fall." Anna suddenly broke off, and lifted her arm to wave across the square.

Liv followed her gaze and spotted two guys heading toward them. The taller of the two was looking right at her, and the way his smile spread slowly across his face as Liv looked up made her stomach crinkle into a little ball and somersault around inside her belly.

"Hey, guys!" Anna stood up and gave each of the two guys a hug in turn. "This is my roommate, Liv."

The shorter guy quickly leaned over and kissed Liv on each cheek. "It's lovely to meet you," kiss, "I'm Francesco Cipriani," kiss, kiss, "from Italy." Liv blushed, in shock from the cheek-kisses. Definitely not the way things work in the Midwest.

"Uh, hi. Olivia Phillips. But call me Liv. From Michigan. Ann Arbor. Near Detroit. You know—Motor City?" Liv laughed, and she could feel her cheeks turning redder. This was so weird. She *never* blushed. But for some reason, she had become a full-on dork in the past day, and kept saying the weirdest things. *Motor City? Where did that come from?* As Liv bumbled through her introduction, the taller guy kept looking at her, and finally stopped her rambling by cutting in to introduce himself.

"I'm Colin Johnstone. From merry old England. God save the queen, yeah?" He winked slyly at Liv. Was he making fun of her?

"I am in the mood for a gelato," Francesco declared loudly in his sugary

Italian accent. With a wave of his hand, he motioned across the square. "Join us?"

As they walked over to Häagen-Dazs—ice cream would have to satisfy Francesco's gelato craving—Liv couldn't stop casting glances at Colin, and thinking about her stomach's little loop de loop. Twice in one day she had fumbled through an introduction—Josh Cameron, and now this guy.

Blaming her dysfunctional social skills on jet lag, she decided to give it another try. She and Colin were walking a few steps behind Anna and Francesco, and Colin didn't seem to be much of a talker. Liv found silence unnerving, and often ended up babbling just to avoid it.

"So . . . where in England are you from?"

"Stratford-upon-Avon." Colin cast a sideways glance at Liv, grinning. "Shakespeare's birthplace."

"I guess that's a little more poetic than Motor City, huh?" Liv giggled. "I've always wanted to go to Stratford. I bet it's beautiful there. So much history. And I just love Shakespeare."

"Are you a tragedy or comedy girl?"

"Comedy. Definitely. They're so fun to watch. I've never actually seen Shakespeare live, just the BBC versions on TV. Hopefully I'll get a chance while I'm in London." Liv paused—was she coming across as a total loser, talking about the BBC and Shakespeare?

When Colin didn't say anything, she decided another question might help. "I guess you've probably seen a lot of theater, being from the Land of Shakespeare?"

Colin nodded. "I actually played Demetrius in *A Midsummer Night's Dream* at school. Twice."

"You're an actor?"

"No. Both times the play was awful. I'm not sure why I even bothered the second time." They both laughed, then more silence. Finally he continued, "There's a show playing now that looks really good. *Deception*, I think. It's a modern version of *King Lear*. Have you heard of it?" Liv shook her head. "If you're interested, maybe we could see if . . ."

Colin broke off midsentence as Anna grabbed Liv's arm and pointed at a billboard overhead. She had burst into a fit of laughter. Josh Cameron's soft brown eyes were twinkling down at them from overhead. As embarrassed as she was about The Incident from earlier in the day, Liv loved that Anna already felt comfortable enough with her to laugh at her dorkiness. The story *was* pretty funny.

Liv's face flushed as she was forced to share the details of her run-in with Josh Cameron once again. She shrugged casually at the end of the story, hoping Colin and Francesco wouldn't see how truly mortified she was.

As Liv followed the others inside Häagen-Dazs—Anna was *still* giggling—she couldn't help but wonder what might have happened if she and Colin had finished their conversation. *Did he just almost ask me out?* Liv wondered, desperate to know what he had been *this* close to saying. Sighing, Liv realized the moment had passed.

Don't Worry, Be Happy

The next morning, Liv woke to find Rebecca staring at her from the kitchen. She was leaning against the edge of the counter, slicing a grapefruit. She greeted Liv with a chirpy "Good day, sunshine!" and an off-key rendition of the classic Beatles' song.

Liv murmured something rude under her breath and rolled over, checking the time. Seven on the dot. She briefly debated whether to give herself the additional fifteen minutes until her alarm was set to go off, but decided against it. Not a good day to risk it, especially since the time difference—and jet lag—was really messing with her sleep schedule.

Liv hustled past Rebecca toward the

shower, eager to get ready and get out of the apartment. She and Anna had avoided saying it out loud last night, but neither of them wanted to show up at their first day of work with Rebecca in tow.

An hour later Liv had squeezed herself into the slightly too small black skirt and light blue T-shirt Anna had lent her the night before. Her green sneakers would have to do—her feet had topped out at a massive size ten in ninth grade, so they were about twice the size of both Rebecca's and Anna's.

With an hour to spare before she had to be at the Music Mix offices, Liv peeked into Anna's room to see if she was ready to go. Anna, only half dressed, made a face and agreed to escort Rebecca to work. "Save yourself," Anna said quietly. "No need for both of us to be stuck with her. But you owe me."

Liv smiled gratefully at her roommate, grabbed her bag, and headed for the door. A coffee at one of the cafés around Oxford Street should make her feel like a real Working Girl. She closed the door behind her and skipped down the stairs.

When Liv arrived at Music Mix at ten to nine, Gloria was singing at the front desk.

She greeted Liv with a little wave and a spin that made her frilly orange dress spin out around her.

"Good morning!" Liv waved back. She was in a great mood—it had been a fabulous morning. She had found a perfect little café just around the corner from the Music Mix offices, and had spent the past half hour relaxing at a quaint table by the window.

Gloria directed Liv to the orientation conference room, where Liv collected a folder with her name on it, then grabbed a free doughnut and cup of tea. As she paged through the folder and munched her doughnut, Liv took inventory of some of the other people entering the room. Some people were *too* cool, and skulked into the room without saying hello (the James Dean guy in leather pants and the snobby purple-haired girl in striped tights were immediately on Liv's "to avoid" list—they didn't even lift their eyes to acknowledge that anyone else was in the room).

Others nodded or smiled in her direction, and looked around uncomfortably. Liv later learned that the pretty Asian-American girl wearing six-inch platform boots just looked grumpy because her shoes were pinching.

Liv was the most impressed with the few people who came in and actually said something. Francesco was the most outgoing, bounding into the room like an electron and kissing everyone. Colin slid into the room behind him, shyly shooting Liv a cute little smile as he took a seat against the wall.

Just a few minutes before nine Anna showed up with Rebecca, who was decked out in an all-white pantsuit with a bright green tank under it. Liv had to admit that it was pretty hot, and definitely daring. Anna didn't look happy, but perked up when Liv pushed a doughnut her way.

Rebecca quickly introduced herself to everyone in the room, starting with James Dean, who was forced out of his one-man world to make eye contact. Rebecca seemed to have learned personal skills overnight, since she made her way deliberately around the room, dishing out compliments and witty little remarks to each person in turn. As she swept past Liv, Rebecca flashed her a gleaming smile. Confused, Liv just stared back.

A loud, raspy sigh from the doorway broke through the awkward small talk, and everyone turned to see who had entered the room. A shortish, thirtysomething guy with tan teeth and pants to match was staring around at the twenty-five people gathered in the conference room. He moved to the head of the table and began to speak.

"Brown. That is what you'll call me. Not Simon. Not Mr. Brown. Just Brown." *So this is Simon Brown,* Liv mused. *Interesting rule.* She wondered if he knew his tooth color matched his name. "I am the head of this program, and I expect that each of you is prepared to work as hard as I do. You have been given an opportunity that many would die for. Consider yourselves lucky to be here." *A bit overdramatic, isn't he?* Liv thought. "Now. Inside the information folder each of you has received, you will find your summer project assignments. You're welcome."

There was a rustling as people sifted through their folders. Liv pulled a sheet of paper from the back of her folder that said "ASSIGNMENT: Olivia Phillips." Scanning it quickly, she spotted what she was looking for. Three little words that would shape the outcome of her summer: "Coordinator, *Hits Parade.*"

Liv couldn't believe it. *Hits Parade* was *the* hottest show on TV. The most fabulous celebrities all swung by Music Mix Europe to promote their latest movies or albums, and the supersexy Andrew Stone played the day's biggest video hits. She read further:

The *Hits Parade* Coordinator will assist in the following:
Audience Control *(Bouncer Liv. Nice.)*
Celebrity Attendance *(What does that mean?!)*
Booking Confirmations
Production Support, including time-management *(uh-oh)*
Segment Writing
Administrative Duties, as needed

"What's your assignment?" Anna was reading over Liv's shoulder. "*Hits Parade*?! That's so great! You are going to have *so* much fun."

Liv agreed. She had definitely gotten lucky. "How about you?"

"Wardrobe in the Features Department. Sounds good to me. I like clothes—" Anna was cut short by a squeal coming from the other side of the table. Rebecca was glowing, and flapping her paper around in the air. She had successfully turned all eyes toward her, and she took the attention as her cue to share.

"Events Team. First Assignment: Josh Cameron Concert! Oh, my dad is going to be so excited." Liv wanted to puke. The thought of listening to Rebecca gloat about the Josh Cameron concert for the next month was sickening. And the way Simon Brown was smiling at Rebecca as she flipped her hair and drawled on was infuriating and kinda gross. He seemed to be taken with her. For that matter, so did all the other guys in the room. Liv had to admit, Rebecca *was* pretty. But she was also so *weird*, and apparently bipolar.

"You. *Hits Parade* Coordinator." *Oh God,* Liv thought, *is Simon Brown talking to me?*

"Yes, Mr. . . . uh, I mean . . . yes, Brown?"

"You're the lucky one this year." Simon Brown huffed out a wheezy laugh. "The *Hits Parade* coordinator has the profound good fortune of serving a unique duty. You'll be at the heart of the action." He paused for dramatic effect. "My assistant."

Was he serious? She was going to be his assistant? Things had just gone from best to worst. Anna grabbed Liv's hand under the table and squeezed. Liv managed a weak smile and muttered a tiny "thanks" before following her new boss out of the room to settle in at her summer desk.

"You. Here." Simon Brown was beckoning to Liv from the inner chamber of his office. She was finally getting settled in at her desk—just outside his door—and pretended she hadn't heard him.

Though she was positioned in a prime location near the *Hits Parade* studio, her "desk" was really just a small table jutting out into the hallway, en route to the coffee machine. She had to suck her belly up against the table edge every time someone needed to get past her. She felt like a tollbooth operator. Maybe she would start charging.

As Brown called out again—only slightly louder this time—Liv decided she really couldn't ignore him, though she couldn't imagine what on earth he needed, considering it was ten o'clock in the morning, she had just fetched him a coffee, and he had been snacking on doughnuts since nine.

He thought he had been sly about the doughnuts, but she had noticed. He was one of those people who took three of the best doughnuts before anyone else had a chance to take one. Inevitably, this meant that some poor, patient soul who had waited his or her turn would get stuck with the crusty, oozy leftover cherry-filled messes while people like Simon Brown gorged on the good stuff.

She slid out of her chair and approached his door. "Yes, Brown?"

"I need you to fetch the contract I just printed." He didn't look up. Liv stood in the door, trying to decide how to tell him that she had no idea where the printer was.

"Uh, Brown? . . ."

"GO, GIRL!"

Yowza. That guy could yell. *Okay, I'll be going now.* Liv smiled slightly and slid back out the door and into the hall. *Well, where to begin?*

Liv shuffled down the hall, gazing into each empty room. The Music Mix office was laid out in a weird, mazelike octagon. Every time Liv thought she had made a complete circle, and expected to see her tollbooth around the next bend, she was in a new wing altogether. She hadn't found a printer, but if anyone ever asked her for the inflatable gorilla costume, she now knew where to find it.

Turning the thirty-seventh corner (how did this building have so many hallways?!), Liv bumped into a familiar figure—Colin.

His expression mirrored Liv's own panicked face. Looking at him, Liv couldn't help but laugh.

"What are you looking for?" she asked, realizing she probably wouldn't be able to help.

Colin held up his hands. "The watercooler. How big *is* this place?"

Liv pointed behind her. "I spotted a watercooler three turns back. Left, then right, then right again. You can't miss it." She giggled. *Am I flirting?* she wondered, noticing that her stomach was doing flip-flops and she had just *giggled*! "What department are you working with?"

Colin scratched his chin. "The Department of One: Andrew Stone. I think my production internship is really just a fancy way of saying 'personal assistant.'" Colin had barely looked at Liv as he spoke—he seemed focused on something just over her shoulder.

"Ooh . . . I'm the *Hits Parade* coordinator." Liv couldn't conceal her enthusiasm. *Yep, definitely flirting.* "We'll be working together!"

Colin shifted from foot to foot and gave her a thin smile. He glanced quickly over Liv's shoulder again. "Right. I, uh, have to get going. See you later, yeah?" He breezed past her and turned the corner.

Did I just say something stupid? Liv wondered, watching Colin hustle off down the hall. Confused, she continued her quest for the printer. The next left led Liv into the round Music Mix front lobby. She stood in the center of the hundred television screens, confused and not sure how she'd gotten there.

"What's wrong, Olivia?" Gloria looked up from her desk. She looked genuinely concerned.

"Hey, Gloria. I'm looking for the printer. Mr., uh, I mean, Brown wanted me to fetch a contract for him. You can call me Liv, by the way. Everyone else does."

"Oh, Liv. I'm so sorry." What did that mean? Gloria's face morphed into a pitying smile. "Brown's printer is in his office. He does this every year. Some sort of power thing."

Liv groaned. "You're serious, aren't you?" Gloria nodded. "Great. That's just great. Thanks for the tip."

"No problem." Gloria shot Liv the same pitying look again. "Let me know if it gets too bad. I think I can help."

Okay, that wasn't exactly reassuring, but

Liv appreciated the offer. "Thanks. Just one more thing—how do I get back to his office?" Gloria laughed, and pointed to one of the many doorways leading out of the lobby.

Back at Simon Brown's office, Liv knocked quietly at the door and made her way inside. He was sitting at his desk, feet up, tan teeth flashing an arrogant smile. She walked over to his desk and plucked five printed pages from the printer in plain view. As she handed them to him, he lifted a glazed doughnut in a salute and pointed to the door.

This could be a very long, very annoying summer.

9 to 5

Liv quickly came to realize that her idealized notion of what a Music Mix internship would be—days joking around with celebrities and nights spent at fabulous clubs and parties—was way off base. The reality was that her days were long, and she rarely got home before nine. A lot of the other interns had been going out after work, but Liv was stuck at her desk most nights until at least eight, finishing busywork for Brown.

Liv spent much of her first week doing meaningless errands: fetching Brown candies every thirty minutes, bringing him paper towels from the "loo," even being called in to press play on his CD player. She had almost no time to eat lunch, let alone mingle in the halls to get details on parties that—even if she did know about them—she would surely need to *sneak* into.

All the interns quickly learned that the Music Mix office was jam-packed with staff employees who thought they were the stars of the music industry, and who did everything in their power to keep interns from thinking too highly of themselves or getting invites to anything. Liv never failed to be impressed by the cool exterior these industry divas maintained. But eventually she realized that they were just as desperate to talk to celebrities as any of the interns were—they were just a little better at hiding it.

Liv's first (disappointing) brush with fame at work was meeting the supersexy Andrew Stone. He dropped by Simon Brown's office Tuesday morning, and on his way to the *Hits Parade* studio he swung through Liv's tollbooth for a cup of coffee. In person, Andrew Stone reminded Liv of a caricature of his TV persona. He was all winks and thumbs-up and smooth hair. Like a good TV star or slimy politician, he stopped to introduce himself and ask a few generic questions.

"Tell me, Olivia," he said, leaning

toward her, all intense and faux interested, "what's *your* music style?" As Liv deliberated, Andrew Stone gazed past her with a polished smile on his face, mouthing "hiiii" to everyone who passed. Liv had to think quickly.

She couldn't really admit the truth to Mr. Pop himself, could she? Would it be a faux pas to reveal that her music obsessions were mostly limited to seventies and eighties stars? She had grown up listening to old albums and light FM radio with her mom, and she couldn't help it—she was addicted. Of course, she had a few current faves (top of the list: Josh Cameron), but the real deal would be an opportunity to time warp and work at Music Mix in the days of ABBA or The Bangles.

She decided to risk it and go with the truth. It looked like he wasn't really listening anyway. "I really like Josh Cameron, but I'm also a big eighties junkie."

"Well, that's great, Olivia." Bingo. Not listening. "I'll see you on set later, yeah?" He pointed little finger guns at her and strutted toward the studio.

On her first afternoon of work Liv found out what one of her assignments—Audience

Control for *Hits Parade*—meant. She was sent into the studio and told to "get things under control." Easier said than done. She opened the door to the small set and was greeted by fifty screaming fans. They had all been herded into a large roped-in area, and were jostling to get to the front of the fence.

As soon as she walked toward the ropes, people began shouting and gesturing at her. She heard it all—from the desperate and jealous "Hey you, how'd you get on that side of the rope?" to "Yo, sexy girl! Hook me up, yeah?" It was Liv's responsibility to quiet the screaming group and get them seated. The task gave Liv a good idea of what a shepherd would have to go through if his flock could talk.

Once she had them in their seats and had turned them over to the amateur stand-up comedian (who was brought on set each day to "get the peeps in the mood"), Liv had to hightail it back to the celebrity holding tank (aka Green Room), where she was responsible for the comfort of that day's guest star.

Initially Liv had been psyched about Star Control—she would get to meet and assist all of the celebrities who came by the set. Wrong-o. Turned out the real stars all have their own entourage, and Liv was left to deal with the overstressed and strung-out Personal Assistants To The Stars.

On Wednesday she had to deal with both Assistant One and Assistant Two to Kevin Landeau. Kevin insisted that there be two liters of completely flat, room temperature Sprite waiting in the Green Room (apparently he had had a rough night on Tuesday, and had already lost his lunch on a panicked and near-tears Assistant Two). That alone wouldn't be bad, but he had insisted that the flat Sprite be in sealed, unopened one-liter bottles.

Liv spent forty-five minutes working with Assistant One on the logistics of flattening the soda, then remelting the safety seal so Kevin could hear the *click* upon opening his Sprite. Liv celebrated her job-well-done later with a flat Sprite in a resealed bottle—Kevin had opted for orange juice instead.

One of the big perks of Liv's position—which was directly related to one of the worst aspects—was her responsibility to clean up after the celebrities and their entourages. Initially Liv had been horrified by the disaster the Music Mix guests left behind in the Green Room. But once she realized that the leftovers were fair game, she came to appreciate the full platters of food and snacks that were almost always sitting untouched in the midst of strewn trash, bottles, and cigarette butts.

Because she rarely had time to grab herself anything for lunch—thanks to Simon Brown's irritability around noon every day—Liv quickly found that the Green Room leftovers were a welcome treat. That first week of work, she pulled Anna out of the wardrobe department several afternoons so they could sneak into the Green Room to devour the tasty leftovers.

"Is it pitiful that we've resorted to eating someone else's trash?" Liv asked Anna as she bit into a forkful of mashed potato Wednesday afternoon. "It just feels wrong—and kinda depressing."

Anna shrugged, stabbing a piece of chicken from the barbecue platter that was laid out in front of them. "Maybe a little pitiful," she agreed. "But delicious."

"True." Liv buttered a piece of corn bread, relishing the taste of American food. She couldn't help but miss some of the comforts of home—she had never been much of a cook, and her internship didn't pay enough to eat out in London. "So, what do you think? We're halfway through the first week. Is Music Mix everything you thought it would be?" Liv and Anna hadn't gotten any time alone to talk since Monday—Rebecca was always within earshot—and Liv was eager to finish the conversation they had started in Leicester Square a few days before.

"Honestly, yes, it is," Anna said passionately. "Liv, this is exactly what I want to do. I mean, I always sort of knew that, but I didn't really want to give up everything to get a job here until I gave it a try. But now that I'm here, I don't ever want to leave."

"That's good, isn't it?" Liv asked, studying her roommate's reaction.

Anna flinched slightly before answering. "Yeah, it's great."

"Okay, roomie, that wasn't very convincing. Want to try that answer again?"

Anna leaned back into the brown leather couch. "I'm glad I know what I want to do. What I'm not happy about is how hard it is to get a job here. And I just don't think I can give everything up—college, scholarships, my mom's dreams—on the off chance that this might work out."

"Anna, your mom's dreams aren't the

same as your dreams. What do *you* want?"

Anna released a deep sigh. "It's not that simple. My mom has done everything in her power to make sure I've gotten everything I wanted my whole life. Now, if I postpone college and pursue this dream, it would be like stabbing her in the back. She really wanted to be an actress when she was younger, but she gave everything up to make sure our family would be comfortable and happy. So I don't think it's fair for me to go all selfish now and say, 'Hey, thanks for everything, but I just don't care what you think or want.'" She broke off, winded. "Sorry, Liv, didn't mean to go off. . . . I'm just frustrated."

"That's okay. I wish I could do something. I feel totally useless." Liv couldn't imagine the pressure Anna was dealing with, and she didn't really know what to say.

"Can we change the subject?" Anna said, flustered. "I really hate talking about it."

"If that's what you want. But know that I'm here for you whenever."

"Thanks," Anna said, smiling. "But I'll be fine. Now, let's talk about something more pleasant."

"Okay . . . ," Liv said.

"I don't mean for that to sound rude—I guess I just need to figure out how to deal with this on my own."

"But you shouldn't have to deal with it on your own. That's what I'm here for." Liv grinned.

"Thanks, Liv." Anna rubbed her belly contentedly. "I should probably get back soon. I'm stuffed anyway."

Liv had completely forgotten about work. She had no idea how long she'd been gone from her desk, but suddenly realized Simon Brown was probably wondering where she was. He never actually wanted her around, but he liked to know she was available whenever he needed her. She usually tried to saunter past his office or cough loudly at least every thirty minutes—it seemed to comfort him. "Yeah, I should get back too. Thanks for lunch."

"No, thank you. Same time tomorrow?"

"It's a date."

That night Liv got home from work at nine, completely pooped and ready for bed. When she walked through the front door, she almost ran into Rebecca, who was sitting cross-legged in the middle of the living room, staring into a giant bright white screen. Liv, stuck somewhere between amused and mildly frightened, stood and stared.

Rebecca turned around and instructed with a sigh, "Oh, Li-uhv, please stop staring. Haven't you seen a sun lamp before?" She went on to explain that the sun lamp had been shipped in by Rebecca's father to "prevent the saddies." Liv just shook her head and holed away in Anna's room until Rebecca announced that she was a "new woman." Liv took that as her cue that it was safe to return to the living room.

"Ah feel so much better," Rebecca purred to Liv as she floated down the hall to her bedroom. "It's so important that I stay sunny and rosy. You know, Li-uhv, Ah'm in charge of the Josh Cameron concert, and there are just so many people who are depending on me."

Liv mustered up a thin smile. *There it is,* she thought. Liv knew this wouldn't be the last time she would have to listen to Rebecca talking about her überimportant role organizing the Josh Cameron concert. They had only been at Music Mix two days, and already Rebecca had taken every opportunity to make sure everyone knew just how critical her internship assignment was.

Anna and Liv were forced to endure the worst of it, since they had to listen to Rebecca ramble on both at work and at home. But what made it worse was that Rebecca seemed to have mastered multiple personalities, and her sweet Texas Belle character from the office was usually replaced by a self-centered, somewhat evil Crazy at home. Anna and Liv had realized their best coping strategy was just to keep their distance.

The unfortunate dilemma was that Rebecca loved to hear herself talk, and often sat in the living room waiting for her flatmates to come home so she could lock them in to one of her famous one-sided conversations. Liv had exhausted her patience for Rebecca's little "quirks" already, but Rebecca didn't seem to get the hint, and things at the apartment continued to spiral from bad to worse.

Exhausted, Liv arrived home from work on Thursday night only to find herself stuck outside the apartment door. When Anna finally heard her banging and came to let her in, Liv discovered that a huge treadmill had made its way into the living room. Liv didn't even bother to question how on earth this monolithic structure had found its way through the door—she knew it had something to do with Rebecca. The monstrosity was stuffed into the corner of the room next to Liv's couch-bed, and it was jutting out over the first seven inches of the front door, preventing it from opening.

Liv carefully approached Rebecca for an explanation, and was greeted with a frustrated sigh. "Oh, Li-uhv, haven't you noticed? The heels in Europe are just so much higher than they are in Texas." Liv stared back at her blankly. Another *don't-you-get-it?* sigh, and Rebecca continued her drawl. "Ah have to practice walking in my heels *somewhere*. You know, Li-uhv, you're welcome to use it. Ah'm sure you're eager to get yourself some pretty heels one of these days—those sneakers are so late nineties."

Ah, yes, Liv thought, once again pointedly ignoring Rebecca's insult. *This is a perfect explanation. She is going to practice walking in heels on a treadmill. Completely logical.*

Liv's bedroom was slowly being taken over by Rebecca's strange, creepy obsessions. And to top it off, a peculiar smell had started to invade the living room, and was getting worse by the day. But Liv didn't have time to figure out what the smell was, since she had finally gotten ahold of Millie

Banks, the westie sweaters owner, who was so excited to get her "darlings" back that she was on her way over to Liv's apartment to make the suitcase swap.

Millie stayed for two hours, giving Liv a full background on the origin of the sweaters. Tired and weirded out, Liv finally got her to leave after handing over her Ann Arbor address so the woman could send Liv a personalized thank-you sweater for the suitcase's safe return.

By the end of her first week of work, Liv was completely worn out. She was frustrated from dealing with Rebecca, cranky from lack of sleep, and angry with her boss. Simon Brown had grown increasingly smug and arrogant throughout the week. He was constantly hurrying Liv out of his office with a harsh "Go, Girl!"

Friday morning Liv woke with a splitting headache and an attitude to match. Rolling out of bed twenty minutes before she had to leave for work, she kicked her leg straight into the treadmill. She released an enormous growl and limped to the bathroom with a huge scowl on her face. The scowl stuck through breakfast and the whole tube ride into work. When she stomped into the office at eight, Gloria looked up from her newspaper and whistled, "Whoa, girl, remind me to stay out of your way. . . ."

Liv stopped for her mandatory morning check-in at the boss's office, where she was greeted by a surly-looking Simon Brown. He pushed his coffee cup across the desk at her, and barked, "Go, Girl!" without looking up from his newspaper. Liv spotted the headline—CHRISTY BITES BACK!—and perked up slightly. Simon Brown only read the gossip pages when he was in a good mood.

Settling into her desk a few minutes later, Liv tried to throw herself into her work. She didn't even bother to look up when she felt someone shuffle to the coffee machine just before nine. She usually muttered a quick hello or chatted for a few minutes (Liv had gotten to know most of the other interns during their morning coffee runs), but that day she just flipped through the pile of nonsense Simon Brown had left on her desk to "deal with," and sucked in her belly to let the person pass.

A few minutes later the same person approached her desk from the other side, coffee in hand. Whoever it was was looking at her, lurking around the side of her chair. Annoyed, she squeezed in even closer to her desk. The person didn't pass. Clearly, whomever it was expected that Liv would move completely out of his or her way.

She had just about had it with Music Industry Divas; the übercool nobodies who worked at Music Mix all thought they were somebody, and treated interns the way they themselves were treated by real stars. It was a vicious cycle. With an enormous sigh, Liv stood up and violently pushed her chair back, shooting the lurker a look that could kill.

"Olivia." Gulp. The lurker was none other than Josh Cameron. "I thought that was you." Liv panicked. *He remembers me? Is that good or bad?*

"Oh. Hi. Um, sorry about that." Liv didn't quite know what she was apologizing for, but she babbled out something to mask her discomfort. What did one say to Josh Cameron? "So, uh, how are you?"

Josh Cameron laughed. "I'm doing well. It seems the same can't be said for you." His eyes twinkled, brightening her mood. "Bad day?"

"Not anymore." *No!* Liv could not believe she had just said that. "I mean, you know, I'm not really a morning person." She smiled slightly. "But I guess you figured out the other day that I'm not really an afternoon person either. Sorry about the revolving door thing." *That's just perfect,* Liv thought. *Remind him about what an idiot you were on Monday. You wouldn't want him to forget.* "So, uh, what are you doing here?"

"I'm meeting Andrew Stone for breakfast."

Yum, Liv thought. *Breakfast of Champions.*

He smiled and continued, "I'm scheduled to play my new single on *Hits Parade* next week."

"Oh, that's great," Liv answered with a very uncharacteristic giggle. *Stop talking NOW!* "Well, I guess I'll see you then—I'm the *Hits Parade* intern this summer."

"I'll look forward to it," Josh Cameron said, smiling. "Are you just in London for the summer?"

Liv stared unblinkingly at him. *Is he actually interested in what I'm saying?* "Yeah, just the summer. Of course, they want me for longer—but I'm in huge demand, so I'm only willing to give them the summer." *What?!* Liv's eyes widened as her mouth spilled out more and more nonsense. *Are you trying to be funny?*

She smiled weakly, torn between wanting him to stay near her forever and wanting him to go so she couldn't humiliate herself any more. "Are you living in London now?" she asked, though she already knew the answer.

"Yeah, just for a while. I find it enchanting. You?"

"Mmm-hmm, enchanting," she repeated. "Sooooo . . ."

He looked down at his watch. A dark curl fell over his right eye. "I should get going."

"Right. Great. Have a good breakfast." Liv lifted her hand in a little salute. She realized she probably looked like a member of Dorks on Parade, and promptly returned her hand to her side.

Josh Cameron laughed, and his eyes lingered on her face for a few nerve-wracking seconds. She instinctively rolled her tongue over her teeth to check for stray food.

"Olivia, you intrigue me." Was he serious? Why was he looking at her like that? "Join me for a night out." He studied her face for a reaction. She stood silent, for once, dumbfounded. The day had just gotten a whole lot better.

"Yeah, sure. Anytime." Liv felt like her

heart had pounded its way right out of her chest and was now thumping away on her desk.

"How's tonight? I'm meeting some friends at a fabulous little club. Come along—you'll have a great time." He scribbled out some details and glided off down the hall. As he turned the corner toward the studio, Liv broke into a celebratory dance. *What just happened?!?* Liv hustled off in search of Anna. This was an emergency.

Life in the Fast Lane

Flushed and sweating and starting to freak, Liv threw her hip against the door to her apartment for the third time and pushed. She was able to nudge it open a full ten inches, and quickly squeezed her arm and right leg through.

As her butt lodged itself into the tiny opening between the hall and the apartment, she was suddenly hit with unsympathetic images of Winnie the Pooh waving and giggling at her from where he was stuck in Rabbit's front door hole. With an unflattering squeeze and a grunt-thrust, Liv eventually wiggled through. Slamming the door shut, she cursed Rebecca and her monstrous treadmill, which was still blocking the front door. *I hate her fit, freakish, stilettoed self.*

Though Liv shouldn't have been surprised at what she found waiting for her in the living room (she realized that she would *never* understand Rebecca), the sight that greeted her was the last thing she ever would have imagined.

The smell that had been growing in the living room—her bedroom—for the past few days had hit an all-time bad. Liv finally understood why. Sitting in the middle of the living room floor, perched atop Liv's silver strappy shirt, was a teeny tiny not-a-dog-not-a-cat creature.

Brown and sort of see-through, the dog (yes, looking again, she could confirm that this odd little creature was definitely a dog) was shaking in its ratlike skin. Its tail, which Liv had to go all squinty-eyed to see, was formed into a curlicue next to its minuscule little butt, perfectly framing the itty-bitty poop that had landed smack-dab in the center of Liv's favorite shirt.

Liv and the dog stared at each other for a good ten seconds, and then Liv broke the standoff to look around the rest of the room. Her eyes scanned from chair to couch to treadmill, taking a quick inventory of the damage. Her pink scarf, her perfect-blue sweater, her backup jeans, her (*noooooooooooo!*) little black dress, her soft green jammie pants, and the silver strappy shirt—complete with curlicue poop—were strewn around the room.

Her suitcase was exactly where it had been that morning, safely zipped and tucked into the corner of the room under Rebecca's sun lamp. But in the corner of her suitcase, there was now an itsy-bitsy hole. This horrid little creature had clearly decided that a thinly chewed hole was the best way to extract the items in her suitcase one by one, just like a tissue box. Her favorite black skirt—which, along with her silver shirt, was on the roster for tonight's date—was half in the hole, half out, winking at her.

Heaving a huge sigh, Liv kicked off her shoes—briefly considering whether this was a safe move with Hell Dog in the living room—and flung herself on her bed-couch. Staring at the dog, which had been following her movements with its eyes, like one of those freaky Victorian paintings, Liv was startled by the clanging of the church bells outside the window. One, two, three, four, five, six, seven, eight . . .

OH NO! She had just an hour until she

was supposed to be back on the tube to make it to her maybe-date-but-*not*-getting-any-hopes-up meeting with Josh Cameron, Superstar.

As she rifled through her suitcase for suitable underwear, Liv caught a whiff of something across the room that was almost more disturbing than her ruined silver shirt—Rebecca's Gucci eau de parfum. *She* was home. Looking up, Liv fixed Rebecca with her angriest stare. Liv suspected she looked more constipated than angry, but it was the best she could do.

"Oh, Li-uhv, A'm just so glad you're getting along with My Rover. Isn't he just the cutest thing you ever did see?" Liv could only imagine that Rebecca was referring to Liv's new best friend, Hell Dog, who was now curled into a brown dot on Liv's shirt. She had, naively, been under the impression that Rebecca was not yet home, as all of Liv's clothes were still strewn about the room as chew-toys. *Ah, yes,* Liv realized, *this is Rebecca. Is it really safe to assume she would do the normal thing and CLEAN UP!?*

"Rebecca . . ." Liv strained to keep her voice calm, hoping that if she played the part of normal, it would somehow inspire normalcy in Rebecca. "Is this your dog?"

Stupid question, but somehow necessary given the circumstances.

"Ah just couldn't stand the thought of being without my perfect little pooch this summer, so I bought myself a new one. You know, they put dogs in a little holding cell for months when you fly them across the ocean? I wouldn't have gotten my puppy back until the end of the summer, so I figured it was just better to get a new one." Rebecca lowered her voice to a whisper and looked sideways at the freakish creature on Liv's shirt. "Isn't he just darling?"

It was official: Rebecca had just crossed yet another line into Crazy. "When did you buy this thing, Rebecca? And where is it going to live?"

Rebecca's eyes frosted over, giving Liv the look that she had grown so accustomed to over the past week. "My Rover has been here since Tuesday. How on earth have you not noticed?" Rebecca sneered, and rambled on. "Ah've already potty trained him. We keep his little wee-wee pad over in the corner, next to the couch. He just piddles on there, and I replace it when he tells me it's time. Ah hope you don't mind." With that, she turned and swooped up the little see-through creature and strutted back to her room.

Was she serious? This creature would be here for the rest of the summer? Peeing in her room? *Well,* Liv thought, as she rooted around in her suitcase, *I guess that explains the smell.*

Glancing quickly at the clock, Liv decided she would have to deal with Rebecca when she got home. Now was not the time to get into a battle. She only had half an hour to find a new shirt and get herself out the door.

She pulled her black skirt the rest of the way out of her suitcase and assessed the damage. No harm done. Balling the skirt, a pink ruffly bra, and her underwear in her arm, she ran to the bathroom and flew through her shower.

Returning to the living room half-dressed, Liv was relieved to see Anna was home and sitting on the couch, looking just as confused as Liv had been a few minutes before. Anna looked at Liv's panicked face, and her eyes darted to the silver shirt still crumpled in the middle of the floor. "Don't ask," Liv blurted out, more harshly than she had intended. "I have to leave in five minutes to meet Josh Cameron and win him over with my charm and grace, and I now have nothing to wear. Help."

Anna stood up, gave Liv a quick hug, and leaned down to press play on the CD player. "Music therapy," she explained, as ABBA's "Dancing Queen" came pouring out of the tinny speakers.

"Dancing Queen" was undoubtedly Liv's favorite song. She sort of liked to think it was her theme song—she *loved* to dance, and loved that you could totally lose yourself on the dance floor. It was the one place where you could reinvent yourself, act goofy and just go with the music.

"Okay," Anna continued, as Liv danced around the living room. "What look are you going for? Sex kitten? Confident seductress? Naive nobody? All of the above?"

"Anna, you're European—just make me look like I fit in."

Anna thought for a second, then darted off to her bedroom closet while Liv shimmied around the living room singing, *"Dancing queen, young and sweet, only seventeen . . ."* Anna returned a few seconds later, holding a silky, shimmery, icy pink sleeveless shirt. "Try this on. It's perfect."

Liv grabbed the shirt and slipped it on over her pink bra. As it slid over her next-to-nothing breasts and down past her slender tummy, Liv could tell it was perfect. It clung in all the right places, revealing just enough that she looked sexy, yet left enough to the imagination that she looked demure and sophisticated.

Anna breathed out a sigh, and grabbed Liv's hands. The two of them spun around the living room, singing along to the last notes of "Dancing Queen." Just as the church bells outside chimed nine times, they collapsed onto the couch in a fit of laughter.

Liv scanned the crowd gathered near the fountain at Piccadilly Circus. As expected, no Josh Cameron. He had told her to meet him at Meat, some new nightclub in Soho.

Liv had secretly hoped that he would surprise her at the subway and escort her there, but she knew she was being totally unreasonable. He was busy and famous. And this was, after all, not a date. She headed across the street and followed the directions Anna had written for her back at the apartment as Liv had strapped herself into the World's Most Uncomfortable Shoes Ever.

Turning onto the club's street, she spotted a long line that snaked around a brown rope outside an unimpressive brick building. A small sign verified that she had arrived at Meat. Uncertain of what to do next, she mingled around the crowd, half in line, half out. There didn't seem to be any real rules or order, since the bouncers were just randomly picking people out of the crowd and ushering them in. Just when Liv's stomach had begun to curl at the idea of standing on the outside of the rope, smiling and flirting in the hope that she would be chosen to enter, a skinny guy in a suit approached her.

"Olivia." He stated her name so matter-of-factly that she immediately nodded and smiled. "He's inside. He asked me to escort you up. Follow, please." Liv had no idea who this guy was, but just assumed that "he" was none other than Josh Cameron.

Liv followed as Skinny Guy made a tunnel through the waiting crowd and toward the door. He snapped twice, and a bouncer quickly pulled the rope aside to let them pass. Liv smiled at the bouncer. He narrowed his eyes and released what Liv could only assume was a growl.

Skinny Guy hustled through the low, narrow entrance to the club, while Liv struggled to stay upright on her shoes. She wondered if her feet were bleeding yet.

She looked around, trying to take everything in as she trailed behind the suited stranger into the main room of Meat. There were about thirty brown leather booths packed around the perimeter of the room, each one lit by a bare, plain white light bulb hanging from a cord extending all the way down from the superhigh ceilings.

The center of the club held a dark, crowded dance floor. Some sort of R&B music was being piped, quite literally, from pipes that extended out of each corner. A bar at the far end of the room was lit by flickering red lightbulbs. The club left Liv feeling creeped out, but she knew she would never admit that to anyone. This was, after all, one of London's hottest clubs, and the site of her first date with *Josh Cameron*.

She and Skinny Guy had made their way past the booths and were now standing in the back corner of the club, next to the bar. They were directly under one of the pipes, so when Skinny Guy turned to say something to Liv, all she could hear was "ung, uh uh snu." She just nodded her agreement (hoping he had asked something reasonable), and followed as he pulled a curtain aside, moved past a bear-size bouncer, and up an unlit staircase.

They emerged into a dim, thickly carpeted room that reminded Liv of her grandparents' small downstairs den. She suddenly wished she were there now, watching movies and giggling with her cousin Luke while their parents played cards and drank cheap wine at the folding table upstairs.

But she wasn't. She was in London. Standing in front of an L-shape couch packed with no less than fifteen people, all of whom were visibly drunk. Judging from the security guards positioned around the room, and the fact that two of the women on the couch had been on the cover of *Us Weekly* last month, Liv could only imagine she had entered some sort of VIP section at Meat.

Skinny Guy disappeared, and Liv suddenly felt very alone. She stood in the doorway for a few minutes, letting her eyes adjust to the low light. She could feel beautiful faces scanning her own, trying to determine why she was here, with them. Among the stars.

Just when she was about to turn and flee, realizing this must all have been a horrible, cruel joke, she spotted Josh Cameron walking through an archway toward her. She could feel the eyes on the couch watching as he breezed up to her and took her face in his hands, giving her a kiss on each cheek.

"You," Josh Cameron whispered in her ear,

"look stunning. Thank you for joining me."

Blushing, Liv allowed him to take her hand. She squared her shoulders and followed as he led her through the archway and pushed aside another velvety curtain that masked a small hidden room. Apparently, this was the VIP section of the VIP section—Liv was overwhelmed.

Josh Cameron gave Liv's hand a quick tug, and he pulled her toward the other side of the curtain, behind him. As she passed through he let the curtain fall back into place, and it knocked heavily into the side of Liv's head. She grunted rather loudly and pushed it off, trying to act natural.

Tucking a stray curl behind her ear, Liv was relieved to see that Josh Cameron hadn't seemed to notice. His attention had turned away from her and on the people crowded into the long, low booth sprawled out in front of them. Liv quickly scanned the faces around the table—she recognized just about everyone, but had never imagined she'd ever be this close to any one of them.

Taking a breath, Liv managed to muster up a thin, nervous smile. Josh Cameron had moved away from her and slid into a corner of the booth, kissing a few people on the other side of the table as he passed. For a few awkward seconds Liv stood alone again. Her heart was racing, and her stomach was flipping up and down.

This was just too much. Not only was she out with Josh Cameron, but she was living in a picture from *People* magazine's Star Tracks section. Directly across from Liv, in the far corner of the booth, It Girl Christy Trimble was wobbily standing on the table in her stilettos, arms out to the sides, dancing with her eyes closed. Several jaw-droppingly gorgeous guys were holding her hands while she flipped her body in time to the music.

Liv noticed that the song currently piping out of the wall was a dance remix of Josh Cameron's recent single, "Split." The song was amazing, and rumored to be inspired by his recent break from Christy Trimble's best enemy, Cherie Jacobson.

As Liv stood there, starstruck, Bethany Jameson—who was, quite possibly, the hottest starlet in Hollywood—nimbly hopped up on the end of the table and danced alongside Christy. Bethany's thong rested a comfy two inches above the ultralow waistline of her Joe jeans. The two women giggled and shimmied, clearly hamming it up for the benefit of the rest of the table. Both of their mouths were wide open, singing loudly and laughing. Josh Cameron looked delighted.

They finished their routine with a quick hug, and Bethany scooted off the table and onto the lap of one of the guys who had, only moments before, been holding Christy's hand. Christy leaned over to plant a quick kiss on Bethany's cheek (obviously there were no hurt feelings about the guy swap) before taking a long sip from her drink.

Josh Cameron motioned Liv toward him in the corner of the booth, and she adjusted her skirt as she slid in beside him. A few of the Star Tracks subjects glanced up briefly to greet her, then went back to their cigarettes and conversations.

"Drink?" Josh Cameron was pouring himself a short glass of vodka from the center of the table, where a buffet of booze sat in icy buckets next to a platter of mixers.

"Oh, um . . ." Liv hadn't really had a lot of opportunity to drink in Michigan. In fact, she had had a total of one nasty incident involving some sort of licorice liqueur that left her facedown on the toilet seat. Her dad had not been impressed, and frankly, Liv hadn't been so impressed with the morning after.

So, she wondered, *is this the time to give it another whirl? With a table full of It Girls and Josh Cameron?* "Hmm, you know, I think I'll pass for now. I had kind of a weird dinner, and my stomach is a little iffy."

Liv realized her excuse sounded pretty lame—and, on second thought, kind of gross—but figured it was better than the alternative. She already had a visual in mind that involved Bear Bouncer dragging a passed-out Liv from the VIP section with her skirt wrapped around her armpits. *Cute.*

"Olivia, you are astoundingly charming. So All-American Girl." Josh Cameron's dimples deepened as he smiled at her. His eyes were deliciously green. Liv couldn't believe she was here, with him. And it *did* seem a little like a date. "Tell me all about *you.*"

"Oh," Liv said, her tongue tied. "Well, what do you want to know?"

"Everything. I want to know what moves you." Josh stared into her eyes, his expression identical to the front of his last CD cover.

Liv was caught between laughing and crying. *Is he serious?* "Well, okay, um, I, ah, I'm from Michigan. Hmm, and uh, I live with my dad?" *Is that a question?! What's wrong with you, Liv? Say something remotely interesting.* "Oh! I know. My mom actually worked as a VJ at Music Mix in New York before I was born. That's something!" Though it was true, Liv wasn't sure why she had decided to mention that, of all things, to Josh Cameron. Although, her mom's music background did make her feel more worthy of sitting at this table, with all of these celebrities.

"I'm in awe, Olivia." Josh Cameron continued to stare at Liv with a poster boy sort of expression. "You are fascinating."

"Okay," Liv said, averting her eyes from his constant stare. "Well, thanks. But tell me about you! I guess I know a lot, but, well, I s'pose a lot of the stuff I read in magazines isn't really true." She laughed awkwardly, hoping to turn the topic of conversation away from herself.

Josh Cameron's eyes twinkled in the low light as he murmured, "It's all true. If you want it to be." Liv swallowed hard, wondering what, exactly, that meant.

In fact, Liv wasn't quite sure *what* she wanted to be true. The Josh Cameron sitting next to her was a little intimidating . . . and rehearsed. She wasn't sure why, but she sort of felt like he was reading from a script. *But,* she reminded herself as he smiled at her again, *you're on a date—in a VIP room—with Josh Cameron! So who cares?*

Liv let herself melt into the booth while Josh Cameron entertained her with stories of his recent tour, gossip about other celebrities, and his plans for the fall. She couldn't believe the life he led. It seemed so fascinating. And as she sat there, he seemed more and more normal. She soon realized that when her mouth was zipped tightly shut, Liv felt a thousand times more comfortable with him.

So for the next several hours Liv let Josh chatter on and enjoyed the insider gossip. As they stood up to dance sometime long after midnight, crowded among the other celebrities, Liv just smiled silently as Josh Cameron leaned in to share the details of his last party at Chateau Marmont. His hands wrapped around her waist, talking all the while—he never even noticed that she hadn't uttered a word.

West End Girls

"Hang on . . . Christy Trimble, Bethany Jameson, *and* C. J. Jackson were there? And you talked to all of them?" Anna stopped to pick up a strand of handmade beads, checking the price.

Liv had promised to spill all the juicy details of her previous night's date if Anna would spend the day wandering around Portobello Road, Notting Hill's outdoor shopping market, with her. Liv had only gotten as far as dishing the scoop on celebrity sightings from Meat, and already Anna was impressed.

"Yeah, they were all there. And it's weird, because Christy is actually really nice. You know how the tabloids say she gets in catfights with people all the time? Well, she was totally friendly to me."

Actually, Liv thought guiltily, *maybe that isn't exactly true.* In reality, most of the other people at Josh Cameron's table had been pretty self-absorbed and virtually ignored her. But Christy had kissed Liv on the cheek when she left and said how "absolutely stunning" Liv looked, which seemed totally unnecessary and had been a really sweet gesture for a stranger.

"Enough. Stop making me jealous with the guest list—get on to the good stuff." They had made their way to a scarf vendor, and Anna poked her head around a rack to find Liv modeling a purple tiger-striped fur.

"Well, dah-ling, it was simply mah-vehlous. . . ." Liv strutted down the aisle with her huge fake fur. "Okay, so there I was, standing alone in the middle of this weird little room with half the models from *Vogue* staring at me. I seriously thought I was going to die. Thanks for the shirt, by the way. It was perfect."

"No problem. You looked hot. Go on. . . ."

As Liv spilled the details of her date to Anna, she relived each second in her head. She could still smell Josh Cameron's cologne, and she could feel his touch on her hand from when he had led her out of the club at the end of the night. He hadn't kissed her, but she sort of suspected he probably would have if Christy Trimble hadn't stumbled out of the club to throw up just as Liv's taxi pulled around the corner.

Liv smiled as she thought about how Josh Cameron had handed her taxi driver a twenty-pound note and opened the door for her, saying, "I'm so glad you could join me, Olivia. I hope you'll be willing to grace me with your presence again soon." *Okay,* Liv thought, grinning. *Maybe that line was a little cheesy. But it was really sweet.*

"Here's the thing," Liv said, watching Anna wrap a long silk skirt around her jeans and model it in the mirror. "The things he said were almost . . . lame . . . sometimes." She cringed. She didn't really want to ruin her memory of the night with a confession that Josh Cameron was less than perfect— but she couldn't withhold any details.

"Ooh," Anna said, lifting her eyebrows. "Do tell."

Liv quickly shared the "I hope you'll be willing to grace me with your presence again soon" line, as well as some of their other conversations. She gritted her teeth after being forced to say it aloud.

Anna burst out laughing. "Are you serious? He actually said that?"

Liv nodded. She had sort of been hoping Anna would say it was sweet and romantic. But who was she kidding? Liv could only hope Josh Cameron would be a lot less scripted if they went out again. After all, she reasoned, he did have to live up to a certain pop star image, and she wondered if maybe his lame, over-the-top lines were partly because he was in London? Maybe his publicist forced him to say junk like "lovely time" and "grace me with your presence." Maybe there was a book of etiquette that celebrities lived by that she just didn't know about?

"I guess the good news is, it sounds like I'll see him again sometime," Liv flashed Anna a quick, coy smile. She leaned down and picked up a fringed lampshade. As she did, she blurted out, "I just don't want to get my hopes up. Let's be realistic. This is Josh Cameron. Isn't it a lot more likely that he'll never call?"

"He'll call," Anna said confidently. "If he's feeding you lines like that, he's obviously trying to be a gentleman. And it sounds like you had an amazing time. Why *wouldn't* he call?"

"You're right." Liv nodded, though she definitely wasn't so sure. But it couldn't hurt to *hope*. Liv linked arms with Anna as they continued their path up Portobello Road. "So," she asked. "What did you do last night? I feel like I've been hogging the last hour with my story. Dish."

Anna began to speak, but was cut off as her cell phone started to ring. She answered, murmuring something in Swedish to whoever was on the other end of the line.

Liv didn't feel too guilty listening, since she couldn't understand anything anyway. All she could tell was that Anna definitely wasn't enjoying the conversation—whomever it was with. After a few more minutes Anna flipped her phone closed and exhaled.

"Who was that?" Liv asked nosily.

Anna look flustered. "My mom," she said simply.

"Everything okay?"

"Fine," Anna said, walking slightly ahead of Liv. Liv got the hint—Anna's mom had called several times since they'd arrived in London, and every time Anna had refused to talk about it. Liv knew something was going on, but it obviously wasn't any of her business. As usual, Anna quickly changed the subject. "To answer your question about last night—I did absolutely nothing. It was super-relaxing, since even Rebecca went out."

"She did?!" Liv couldn't hide her surprise. *Who would date Crazy?* "With who?"

"You're not going to believe this, but . . . Colin!"

Liv's stomach sank. "Are you serious?" she asked, hoping Anna was joking. There was still a little part of her that couldn't stop thinking about the sweet, kind, funny Colin she had met on her first day in London. She hadn't seen that guy resurface since that first evening in Leicester Square, but there was *something* about him that made her insides clench every time she saw him. But, she reasoned, if Colin was dating Rebecca, maybe she had gotten the wrong impression.

"Completely serious," Anna said. "I have no idea how it happened, but I guess they've been hanging out. I'm trying to get the dirt from Francesco, but he claims there's nothing going on."

This just didn't seem right. But maybe Rebecca was more normal around Colin than she was around her and Anna. She had mastered multiple personalities, so maybe there was a sweet, seductive side that Liv just hadn't witnessed yet. "Well, this should be interesting to watch, if nothing else."

Anna nodded. "Yes, indeed."

"*Oh, Li-uhv*, why are you so pushy?"

Rebecca was not taking Liv's anger about My Rover's behavior very well. In fact, she had interpreted Liv's request to move Hell Dog's wee-wee pad out of Liv's bedroom as a personal attack. Liv was still astonished that Rebecca hadn't yet apologized for the whole curlicue poop incident from the previous evening, but as Rebecca angrily yammered on, Liv realized that there would be no apology forthcoming.

"Sometimes, Olivia," Rebecca continued, "people need to *compromise*. You are living with three other people now—me, My Rover, and Anna—so maybe you should stop being so concerned about you, and think about other people's feelings for once. *Ah mean*, how do you think My Rover feels about all of this?" Rebecca stopped chiding for one dramatic moment, then stormed on. "He's devastated, Liv. Just devastated. He's ashamed that his wee-wee pad is causing you problems. He's been curled up in his little blanky in the corner of the couch all afternoon, pouting. Doesn't that just break your heart?"

"Does *what* break my heart?" Liv blurted out, astounded. "The fact that your dog is currently curled up in *my* blanket on *my* bed? Yes, that does break my heart!" Liv took a deep breath and continued. "Rebecca, I am very sorry that your dog is devastated. But I think it's reasonable for me to ask that you find a nice, cozy place for his *potty mat* in *your* room. Sound good?" Liv crossed her fingers, hoping for a break.

"Oh, Li-uhv." Rebecca swept her see-through dog into her arms and sidled down the hall. "Ah pity you." With that, she delicately closed her bedroom door and left Liv alone in her living room.

Liv rolled her eyes and fell back on the couch. Clearly, logic and rational discussion weren't going to work. Liv leaned over the arm of the couch, gathered up Hell Dog's wee-wee pad, and strolled down the hall. She plunked the mat right in front of Rebecca's door and returned to the living room.

A few seconds later Anna poked her head out of her bedroom door. "Is it safe?" she mouthed, tiptoeing over to the couch.

"Feel like going out tonight?" she whispered conspiratorially.

"Did you hear that conversation?" Liv grumbled. "I'd rather spend the evening at Simon Brown's flat than deal with another second of Little Miss Don't-Mess-with-Texas in there."

"Great!" Anna squealed, before quickly covering her mouth. "I just got off the phone with Francesco," she continued, whispering. "Apparently Colin got tickets to a show from Andrew Stone earlier this week. It's some hot new band that's playing at a club in Shoreditch. I've already laid out a shirt for you on my bed. Throw on your cute jeans, and let's get moving."

"You . . . and I. Were meant . . . to be. But you . . . took the low road, baby . . ."

This is absolutely awful. Liv quickly glanced around the club to see the reaction on other people's faces. Nodding heads and swaying hips surrounded her. *Apparently, I just don't get it.*

Liv had been feeling that way for the past two hours—basically, since she and Anna had met up with Colin and Francesco outside Presence. Presence was a dimly lit, Asian-inspired club that reminded Liv of a

China Buffet restaurant. Slightly tacky and oddly fragrant, it gave her the willies.

Anna had seemed completely at ease walking into the club, but Liv felt her stomach clenching much like it had when she'd arrived at Meat the night before. The scene was very much *not* Michigan. Tiki lamps dotted the walls, and people lounged on the floor around a battered stage.

As the foursome had moved farther into the club in their quest for a table, Liv's eye was drawn to an enormous fish tank decorating the center of the room. After looking more closely, Liv could see human faces peering back at her from *inside* the fish tank. She had stared at the faces until Colin leaned over and explained with a grin, "Men's room."

"Of course," Liv had responded, horrified. She found it disconcerting that everyone else was acting so normally. Were they oblivious to the fact that there was an enormous see-through *toilet* slicing through the center of the room?

Now, several hours later, Liv was stuffed between Anna and a large bearded man, listening to—quite possibly—the *worst* music she had ever heard. As Liv's eyes wandered around the club for *any*one else who shared her pain, she felt a hand brush her arm. Tensing, she turned. Colin was leaning forward, a smile teasing the corners of his mouth.

Liv felt her chest tighten as his mouth moved toward her ear. "This really is astoundingly awful, yeah?" His lilting English accent made the criticism sound almost dignified. Liv nodded, then started to laugh. "Shall we head out, then?" he asked. Giggling uncontrollably now, Liv nodded again. She grabbed Anna's arm while Colin pulled Francesco toward the door. Outside, Liv burst into laughter.

"What's so funny?" Anna asked. "Why did we leave?" Laughing, she continued, "Is it because of the song about pancakes?"

"Hmm, I sort of liked that one," Francesco mused, then chuckled. "I think the song that really got to me was the one about getting stuck in a scuba suit. It was very romantic, but also odd."

"Okay, so I wasn't the only one who didn't *get* that?" Liv asked, still laughing. "Colin, you got those tickets from Andrew Stone?"

Colin nodded. "I'm starting to think my boss may have been playing a joke on me. . . ."

"Hey, Liv." Anna was grinning in Liv's

direction. "Maybe you should suggest a few of those lyrics to Josh Cameron. After last night I'm sure he would be happy to get your creative input."

Liv shot her roommate a faux-angry look. "Very funny," she said. Blushing, she quickly gave the group a shortened recap of her date while they walked toward a fish and chips shop for a late-night snack.

"So you are . . . dating Josh Cameron?" Francesco asked in his soft Italian accent. Though he was asking Liv the question, he looked at Colin as he waited for the answer.

Liv shrugged. "No. I don't think you could call it that. But I guess I'll see what happens." Francesco was still looking at Colin, and Liv sensed there was some weird unspoken thing going on, but she couldn't figure it out.

You hardly even know Colin, Liv thought, rationalizing the awkwardness. *He's obviously not interested—he's hanging out with Rebecca! Besides . . . Josh Cameron, Colin, Josh Cameron, Colin . . . Do you really have a choice if there's even a* chance *with Josh Cameron?*

Liv linked arms with Anna, still perplexed by the exchange she had just witnessed between Colin and Francesco. *Am I missing something?* she wondered. *Am I making a huge mistake?* She studied Colin's form strolling down the sidewalk in front of her. He stopped and turned, holding the door to the fish and chips shop open. As a smile spread across his face, Liv desperately tried to unravel the knot that had formed in her stomach. *Uh-oh,* she thought, recognizing the crush feeling all too well. *What am I going to do?*

I Will Survive

Simon Brown's feet rested comfortably atop his desk, his coffee cup empty next to them. He was trying to read the morning paper but was distracted by his empty mug.

Glancing at the door every few seconds, Brown briefly considered slipping his feet off the desk and back into the loafers sitting at his side. He was tempted to fetch *himself* a fresh coffee. But he was comfortable, and he enjoyed the fact that he had an excuse to be angry.

It was eight fifteen Monday morning, and Liv was running late.

As she hustled past the security guard and swept past Gloria in reception, she knew she was in for it. Simon Brown did not tolerate lateness, and his morning coffee was not a game. Liv knew she had effectively *"ruined his life"* by showing up fifteen minutes late.

After throwing her bag and umbrella in a heap at her tollbooth, Liv adjusted her skirt and cautiously approached his door.

"Good morning, Brown. Did you have a nice weekend?"

"I'm not sure if you're stupid or arrogant," Simon Brown mumbled, "but I believe we agreed that eight would be an appropriate starting time?" He didn't lift his head from his morning paper, but Liv could feel his beady little eyes narrowing.

"Now. You," he continued. "I will take a coffee, as usual, and ask if you might be so kind as to prepare the conference room for our Monday morning meeting. Will you need help, or do you think you'll be able to manage?" Brown tilted his face up and flashed a tan smile in Liv's direction. She suspected there wasn't a lot of love behind those pearly not-so-whites.

"Not a problem, Brown. Consider it done."

"I'll consider it done when I have a coffee in my hand. Please don't play games with me." As Liv made her way to the door,

Brown continued. "Now, I assume you sent a meeting reminder memo out to all interns on Friday?" *Hello. Memo?!* "All interns *will* be in the conference room at ten?"

This was the first Liv had heard of either the Monday morning meeting or a memo. "Yes, sir—uh, Brown. We'll all be there! I'll be back with your coffee in a sec."

"Go, Girl!"

As Liv zipped through her tollbooth toward the coffee machine, she racked her brain for any memory of this meeting.

She couldn't come up with even a glimmer of what he was talking about. But last Friday had been a little scattered, considering the evening's "date" with Josh Cameron. As she pressed the brew button on the coffeepot, Liv formulated a plan. With Gloria's help, she should be able to catch most of the interns on their way in. A little help from her friends should guarantee word would get out to the rest. No worries.

"As I've already made clear, each of you is living a once-in-a-lifetime experience. I trust you have no complaints?" Brown scanned the meeting room, and looked pleased to see no heads shaking.

Amazingly, word about the meeting had

spread in twenty minutes flat. Liv had filled Gloria in on the situation, and Gloria had immediately kicked into action. Apparently, the "forgotten memo" trick was a regular in Simon Brown's book of intern gags. Gloria had a plan to counteract this and several other Brown crises. Liv was grateful to have Gloria's help—she imagined the receptionist could get pretty feisty, and she wouldn't want to be on her bad side.

After pausing to ensure all twenty-five interns were focused on him, Brown continued his pep talk. "You may not believe it, but this summer will soon be even more remarkable for one or several of you." Brown's mouth curved into an uncomfortable smile. "This year, each of you will have the opportunity to participate in Music Mix's VJ for a Day contest. With the cooperation of our very own Andrew Stone, we have arranged an audition date later this summer. This will be your opportunity to show us if you have what it takes to be on-air talent, or if you can effectively work behind the scenes on one of the production teams.

"Perhaps . . . ," he continued, "if you really blow us away, there may be a job offer for one of you at the end." Brown puckered his lips and smugly sat down.

Andrew Stone, who had been slouched seductively in the corner, stood up and cleared his throat. "Right. Are you ready?" He paused. Liv was temped to pump her arm in the air and shout out, "Yea-uh!" but figured it wasn't a good bet.

"The auditions will be held in August, and the winning team's segment will go on the air that same day. We'll include it as part of the *Hits Parade* lineup." Andrew Stone was beaming. "I'm sure you've all watched my stuff, so you know the deal. Your role, as VJ, will be to hold the audience's attention throughout the video countdown, and keep them coming back for more. Obviously, I've mastered it—feel free to look at some of my earlier work for examples of great novice VJing. You can do a skit, a game—hey, you can strip if you like—just come up with the best gimmick, and prove that you've got what it takes to be on the Music Mix VJ team. Someone in this room will be a Music Mix VJ for a Day. Excited?"

Liv glanced around the room. This was crazy. One of these people could possibly *be* a Music Mix VJ? Now this—*this*—was exactly what she had been hoping this internship would be. She wanted to do *real* TV work— not just Simon Brown's grunt work.

Everyone was grinning ear to ear, and chattering nervously with the people next to them.

Simon Brown quickly wrapped up the meeting and sent all the interns back to their departments. As Liv headed off to her tollbooth, Anna caught up with her.

"Liv, we are going to rock at this. Team?"

"Of course!" Liv grinned. "What are we going to do? I'm up for anything except getting naked—that's going a little far, even for me." Anna laughed as Liv quietly mocked Andrew Stone's stripping suggestion.

"Liv, I think this might be my chance," Anna said seriously as they moved away from the conference room.

"You think if we won the audition, you could get a job offer?" Liv inquired. She wasn't so sure—Brown didn't seem like the type of guy to make things so simple.

"I know he said it was only a possibility, but I just have a feeling. We *have* to win this competition. You're in, right?" Anna looked so desperate.

"Absolutely." Liv gave her roommate a quick, reassuring hug—she knew how much Anna wanted this. "We *will* get you a job."

As Liv and Anna wandered back through the halls, they could hear Rebecca's distinctive voice behind them. Liv stopped and glanced over her shoulder. Rebecca was walking with Colin and discussing the competition. From the sound of it, Rebecca was pretty sure she would win. And she seemed to think it would boost her chances if she told everyone how much she wanted it.

"We *must* work together on this, don't you think?" Rebecca purred to Colin. "Of course, I have to focus on the Josh Cameron concert first—Joshie is so sweet, so I just want to make sure everything's perfect—but after the concert we'll focus every ounce of our energy on this. What do you say, Colin?" Rebecca giggled, casting Liv a sidelong glance as she linked arms with Colin and slid past Liv and Anna down the hall.

Colin murmured something quietly in response, and Liv felt a little like throwing up. Though Liv had begun to get used to the idea of them dating—Rebecca and Colin had spent all day Sunday together, and Rebecca had made sure Liv and Anna were informed about *all* the details—Liv felt queasy seeing them together. She couldn't shake the feeling that had swept over her when her eyes had met Colin's on

Saturday—but obviously, she was the only one who had felt something. So she was doing everything she could to forget it.

"Jemma *always* meets and greets one fan at appearances. It's the way she keeps it real." Jemma Khan's personal assistant, Sam, was standing at the door of the *Hits Parade* studio. Liv was inside the studio, arranging ropes and chairs for that afternoon's show.

Sam had been trailing Liv most of the day, announcing things at random. Liv knew Sam wanted her to do something with each of these announcements, but she was never quite sure what. She had found that if she waited a second, Sam would usually expand. This time was no exception.

"Soooo," Sam said slowly, "can you find a fan for Jemma to spend a few minutes with? You know, to keep it real with . . ." Liv smirked. Sam had delivered that line with complete sincerity. She had clearly been well trained.

"No problem, Sam." Liv pulled the velvet rope taut in front of the audience seats. She had to make sure it was clear that the rope was a barrier—yesterday she had come into the studio just before taping to find a girl sitting in the center of the *Hits Parade* stage. Liv had to literally drag the girl back into the fan section, where she spent the rest of the show sulking and shouting out obscenities. Eventually the girl was removed from the set, but not before grabbing a nice, thick chunk of Liv's hair. The audience control portion of Liv's job was truly a delight.

"Liv, you're the best," Sam gushed, relieved she didn't have to mingle with the "regular people" to find her boss a token fan. "Please make sure you don't find a Crazy. Or it's my butt on the line—you know how it is."

"Yes, Sam," Liv sighed. "I know how it is."

And she did.

Liv had spent much of the past week getting to know the *Hits Parade* fans. She studied them, trying to figure out how *not* to act in a celeb-dense situation. The *Hits Parade* audience was a captivating combination of several types of fans—Criers, Desperate Wannabes, Psycho Stalkers— many of whom fell into the "Crazy" category. But she knew who Sam was looking for—a Regular Fan.

Regular Fans were the non-Crazy folk. Regular Fans usually consisted of tourists, preteens, and groups of girlfriends. They were psyched to be on set, and respected the rules of the game.

The Criers could almost be considered Regular Fans, but not quite. They were the people who got teary-eyed and panicky when they could sense that a star was near. The Criers didn't need to *see* the star—it was enough to know the star was close. The thrill of being in or near the Music Mix building could even send them over the edge. Most days Liv found a Crier in meltdown mode just outside the studio. They were unable to go any farther, suddenly overcome by the possibility of a brush with fame.

The Desperate Wannabes, on the other hand, terrified Liv. Desperate Wannabes dressed and acted like stars, and embodied a presence that shouted, *I'm Somebody!* They went to abnormal lengths to get into the studio, because they felt they *deserved* to be there. And they wouldn't take no for an answer. Every moment in the audience was an opportunity to be "discovered," and Liv would *not* be the one to take that away from them. Liv had seen one Desperate Wannabe actually brush off a C-list reality TV star because the reality star was "beneath" her.

The star's ego was severely damaged, and Liv had to do some major pampering to prevent a diva moment.

The real Crazies were the classic nut job fans—the Psycho Stalkers. On Tuesday one Psycho Stalker had found his way into a performer's dressing room and rested nonchalantly on the couch. When the star had returned from rehearsal, the Psycho Stalker was sitting there, sipping a Perrier, and chatting with the star's dog. He greeted the star with a chirpy "g'day," then continued his conversation with the dog. Needless to say, security had him removed from the area.

In addition to audience control, Liv had spent her week attending to various errands for Personal Assistants to the Stars, like Sam. Most of the errands, she guessed, were tasks being shirked by said Personal Assistants so they could grab a cigarette, a coffee, and a break. Liv's job description had listed "celebrity attendance" and "booking confirmations" as her responsibilities; she was pretty sure that didn't mean "dog walker" or "stain remover." However, she was quickly realizing that *Hits Parade* coordinator made her the go-to girl whenever a dog "piddled" on the Green Room carpet or a cup of organic chai spilled on a cashmere tank.

The only thing getting Liv through the workweek was the fact that Josh Cameron was scheduled to perform on *Hits Parade* on Friday, and he had been around the studio all week rehearsing. She hadn't seen or talked to him since their maybe-date the weekend before, but she had spotted him from afar, chatting with Andrew Stone or rehearsing in the *Hits Parade* studio. She was dying to know if Josh Cameron had been genuine when he told her he wanted to see her again.

As she passed the studio one day, casually peeking to see if Josh Cameron was around, Liv spotted Colin and Andrew Stone in a conversation. She paused, waving to Colin through the window. He looked up, ignored her, and turned in the other direction. Andrew Stone glanced over his shoulder to see who was at the window, and—without the slightest hesitation or acknowledgment—returned to his conversation with Colin. Feeling like a total nuisance, Liv hustled down the hall and back to her tollbooth.

Liv wanted to believe she was imagining it, but almost every time she had seen Colin in the office that week, he had quickly turned and gone in the other direction. She wasn't sure what she had done to offend him, but she got the impression that he was avoiding her. Between Colin and Josh Cameron, Liv was starting to wonder if she was invisible.

One afternoon she ran into Colin at Tully's, the coffee shop around the corner from the office, and lingered long enough so they could take the short walk back to Music Mix together. He stayed mostly silent as they made their way up the escalator, and as soon as they passed Gloria's desk he quickly hustled off, casting glances over his shoulder and generally acting weird. *Rebecca must be getting to him,* Liv thought, smiling.

When Friday, the day of Josh Cameron's *Hits Parade* session, finally dawned, Liv's nerves were out of control. She was frustrated that she hadn't talked to him all week, but she knew he was busy promoting his single. There were a million good explanations. So, positive attitude in hand, Liv dressed herself in her Friday best and glided off to work, hopeful that today would be the day.

She arrived at her tollbooth a few minutes before eight and found a note from Simon Brown that read:

2 Sheepskin throws
14 Red Bulls (NOT 13)
Stuffed pig

After rereading the note a few times, Liv finally gave up and walked to the lobby to find Gloria. Gloria was sitting at her desk, twisting one long dreadlock around her finger while she sang along to "Split."

"Hey, girl. What'd he do this time?"

Liv passed the note across Gloria's desk. "I need you to help me translate. Any idea what this means?"

Gloria glanced at the note, and then passed it back. "Josh Cameron is on *Hits Parade* today?"

"Yeah," Liv responded. "Why?"

"That's his usual request. Brown must want you to get the Green Room ready. You can get the sheepskin throws from Andrew Stone and buy the Red Bull at the market on the corner." Gloria paused, then reached under her desk. "And here"—she triumphantly held up a worn purple pig—"is your stuffed pig." She smiled. "Good?"

Liv just nodded. "Thanks. Again." This was too weird. Why did Gloria have a stuffed purple pig under her desk? And more important, how scary was it that Josh Cameron wanted a stuffed pig waiting for him in the Green Room when he arrived?

Liv spent the rest of the morning preparing the Green Room and getting the studio ready for that afternoon's audience. Her stomach did a little backflip each time the door to the Green Room opened or someone entered the *Hits Parade* studio— she was constantly on pins and needles waiting for Josh Cameron to arrive.

Finally, around one, Josh Cameron breezed into the studio. A small entourage of PR people, personal assistants, and a crew from the *Star* accompanied him. He glanced in Liv's direction, and then instructed one of his assistants to clear the room so he could rehearse in private. Liv and several other interns were shooed out of the way as Josh Cameron began singing his scales.

Around two, just before *Hits Parade* went on air, Liv was summoned to the Green Room. *This is it,* she thought. She was bummed that Josh Cameron hadn't said hello earlier, but she figured things had been hectic. *Whatever,* she thought. *Now is better than never.*

When she knocked at the door a few minutes later, Skinny Guy (her buddy from Meat) greeted her. He was wearing a suit again.

She could see Josh Cameron in the background, strumming his guitar on the couch. He briefly looked up, gazing through Liv with a blank expression. She smiled in his direction, but Skinny Guy moved slightly to block her view.

"Yes," Skinny Guy began. "He will need Gummi Bears and a toothbrush. That will be all."

Liv stared for a moment. *Is this for real?* The look on Skinny Guy's face suggested that yes, this was for real—and that she had better hop to it. Liv nodded, casting a quick glance over Skinny Guy's shoulder, then turned to leave. She headed out onto Oxford Street in search of Gummi Bears.

Forty-five minutes later, Liv sat at her tollbooth, weary and disappointed. She had delivered the requested items to the Green Room and received nothing more than a short thanks from Skinny Guy. No "hello, nice to see you, have a good one," nothing. She was near tears and incredibly embarrassed.

She didn't know what she had expected. Did she want Josh Cameron to embrace her and sing to her, announcing their love to the *Hits Parade* audience? *Um, no. Creepy.* But she had expected a glimmer of recognition from him. At the very least, he could have said hello. She was humiliated that she had apparently read too much into their date. She should have realized how stupid she was being—really, did she think that she and an international superstar would start dating? Seriously, why would he waste his time with a nobody from Michigan?

Liv was pulled from her depression by Simon Brown's loud bark. "You. Here." She dutifully made her way to his open door.

"Yes, Brown?" She could barely muster up the energy to be polite.

"I need my sweater." *Details? No? Okay . . .* "Go, Girl!"

Liv trudged off in search of Brown's sweater. She hadn't the faintest idea where he could have left it, but he rarely dragged his lazy butt farther than the *Hits Parade* studio or the Green Room, so she figured she might as well start there. As Liv passed the studio, she could hear the rumblings of the crowd. Checking her watch, Liv noticed that there were still a few more minutes left in the show—she would have to come back. Postshow crowd was the *last* thing she could deal with today.

She turned right and moved toward the Green Room. As she approached the door, she could hear a few faint guitar chords coming from inside. Knocking softly, Liv pushed the door open.

Josh Cameron was alone, sitting on the couch and strumming his guitar, looking more fabulous than ever. One dark curl brushed his cheek. He looked up and smiled. "Olivia."

Liv braced herself. So he did remember her. What was *with* him? "Hi. Um, great show." *Great show? He ignored you all day, made you feel like a complete idiot, and sent you off on errands to fetch little treats. And all you can say is "great show"?*

"Olivia, I need to apologize. I haven't been myself today. I'm afraid I've given you the wrong impression." He laid his guitar on the couch and stood up to approach her. He leaned forward to kiss her on the cheek. As he did, Liv could smell the cologne that had haunted her all week. *Mmmm. Yummy.* "Have you had a good week?"

"Me? Oh, um, yeah. Sure. It's been . . . well, it's been okay. A little strange, maybe, but you know . . ." Liv trailed off. There she went again. Blah, blah, blah. "So . . ."

"Olivia, I feel terribly about how I've treated you today. I'm afraid you must hate me."

This guy is good, Liv thought, smiling. "Not at all. Don't worry about it. I know you're busy and distracted."

"That's not an excuse. But you understand, don't you?" Josh Cameron smiled, exposing his dimples. "I've been looking forward to seeing you all week. I hope you know that."

Liv swallowed. Hard. She did not know that. "I've been looking forward to seeing you too. I had a great time on Friday. Thanks again for inviting me. And don't worry about today. Really. I understand." *Shhhh, Liv,* she begged herself. *Stop now.*

"Listen, let me make it up to you. Are you free tonight?" Liv nodded. She was now. "Would you join me for dinner?" Liv nodded again.

Just then she spotted Simon Brown's sweater sitting atop the chair in the corner. *Thank you, Simon Brown,* she thought, grinning. *One of your meaningless errands has finally been worth it.*

Wake Me Up Before You Go-Go

Please don't let this be happening to me.
Please don't let this be happening to me.
Please don't let this be happening to me.

Like a mantra, Liv repeated her internal plea again and again. She stared at the unforgiving bathroom door, studying its blank façade. She pressed her nose up against the opaque glass door and tried to get a view into the exterior of the hotel room.

There had to be an emergency door handle somewhere. *Come on . . . where is it?!*

Pushing gently against the muddy glass, Liv studied her wiggly reflection in the door. She suddenly pictured herself dying a slow, miserable death, alone in Josh

Cameron's hotel bathroom. She could see the *Sun* headline: STRANGE GIRL DIES HORRIBLE, SQUISH-FACED DEATH IN AN ATTEMPT TO WOO JOSH CAMERON. Liv peeled her face off the door's glass. Smushing her face against the door was not helping matters.

"Abracadabra!"

"Open Sesame!"

"Supercalifragilisticexpialidocious!" *Oops. That's something else.*

Trying to think of few more magic words, Liv slouched against the wall and stared at the indigo toilet taunting her from the opposite wall in the dark red bathroom.

When Liv had turned up for her date with Josh Cameron that evening, things had seemed so promising. The plan was to have a quiet dinner in his hotel suite. Apparently, Josh Cameron was fed up with the paparazzi and had been trying to lay low. That was fine and dandy with Liv—she was more than happy to check out a superstar suite at the Ñ Hotel.

The Ñ was famous for its übercool, sparse rooms and state-of-the-art technology. Retinal scanners instead of keys. Voice-activated elevators. Automated dumbwaiters that dispatch room service orders through little tunnels in the walls ("Like a drive-up

ATM!" Liv had lamely proclaimed when their champagne had arrived).

And touch-free bathroom fixtures, which were, Liv now realized, *not* a good thing.

When she had arrived, Josh Cameron had greeted her at the door and ushered her into his suite. He had produced a bottle of champagne from the room service receiving berth, and poured deep glasses for each of them. The bubbly champagne shot straight to Liv's head, combining with nerves to make her dizzy and flustered.

After a few minutes of awkward conversation about his suite (during which, Liv recalled with a twinge of discomfort, Josh Cameron had smiled smugly at each of Liv's gushing remarks and nodded, saying, "I know, I know," over and over again), Liv had excused herself to the bathroom.

Which is where she remained, ten minutes later.

Near tears, she decided to give it one more go. She could only imagine what Josh Cameron was thinking, waiting for her out in the suite. Really, what could a person do for ten full minutes in the bathroom? It was not a pretty thought.

Liv stood up and moved toward the door

again. Its smooth, glassy surface was unmarred by a handle. She studied the walls around the door for the umpteenth time, looking for any opening device. She ran her hand along the tiles, stopping when she felt one tile tilt slightly. It looked just like the rest of the bathroom's dark red tiles. Hopeful, Liv gave it a hesitant poke. The door swooshed open, revealing the interior of Josh Cameron's hotel suite. Liv released the breath she had been holding and stepped out of her bathroom prison.

"Well, hello there." Josh Cameron swept across the room toward Liv, holding her champagne flute in his hand. "Everything all right?" He tilted his head and smiled.

Liv took a deep slurp of her drink and felt her face blush a bright crimson. Whether it was from embarrassment or the champagne, she didn't know. "I'm amazing," she said, feigning a seductive purr. As her voice garbled out, she realized she sounded pretty stupid, and decided not to experiment with seduction again.

"I'm going to guess," Josh Cameron said, lifting his glass in a toast, "that you had some problems with the door. Am I right?" Liv nodded sheepishly. "Not to worry," he continued. "It took me a while to find my way around in here. The first time I ordered room service, I waited for two hours not realizing my order had been cooling in the wall panel the whole time."

Liv laughed, and—unsure of what to say—drained her glass.

"Tell me, Olivia," Josh Cameron said, filling her glass with more bubbly trouble. "What is it that makes you so incredible?"

"Well," she began, her confidence bolstered by her glass and a half of champagne. "Perhaps it's my understated grace and elegance?"

Josh Cameron's dimples deepened. "Let's see . . ." He took Liv's arm and led her to a chaise in the corner of his suite's living room. "I don't think it's that. But you are exceedingly charming."

For obvious reasons, Liv cracked up. *Charming?* Liv's champagne was dancing around inside her head now, causing her words to spill out a few seconds before she had a chance to consider them. "What *do* you see in me? Seriously? I mean, I've done nothing but humiliate myself every time I've seen you, and yet you insist on calling me 'charming.'"

Josh Cameron laughed. "It's just *that*, Olivia. I admire your incredible ability to say everything that crosses your mind. It's refreshing to meet a real girl." He took her hand and leaned in close. "You're different."

Liv sucked in her breath. "I see." Her hand was resting lightly in Josh Cameron's palm, sweating. She regretted not swiping Lady Speed Stick across every exposed surface of her body. *Is he holding my hand? Is this real?*

As Josh Cameron stroked the top of Liv's hand with his thumb, she relaxed into the chaise. "Can I ask you something?" she asked, smiling slowly.

"Anything."

"Why did you ask for a stuffed pig at Music Mix?" Liv giggled.

Josh Cameron leaned in closer. She could feel his breath on her cheek as his lips moved toward her ear. "Because," he said with a smile, "it's always fun to see how far people will go to make me happy."

Liv giggled again. In her slightly drunk state, his answer made her laugh. "So the purple pig was what, like a challenge or something?"

"I guess you could say that. Now, Olivia," Josh Cameron pulled away from her and smiled. "I just heard our dinner arrive. Shall we?"

"Let's," she said with a nod. She was

starting to feel sleepy, and was suddenly nervous that if she didn't get some food in her stomach, she could be curled up in the corner passed out in a matter of minutes. Or worse, she would be forced to use the bathroom again. And Liv definitely didn't want to get trapped in there a second time.

Josh Cameron led her to the table that had been set for them in the corner of the suite. Liv studied the table, counting no fewer than seven forks and four plates in front of each of their seats. *I guess I should have watched* Pretty Woman *more carefully— the fork lesson would have come in handy.*

"A toast." Josh Cameron was standing at Liv's side, one hand resting on her shoulder, the other holding his glass toward her. "I feel so lucky to have met you. To what's next," he finished, squeezing her shoulder.

Liv lifted her glass to her lips, but carefully monitored her intake. "To what's next," she repeated, groaning inwardly at his lame line. "Josh, do you always use canned lines like that?" Liv's left hand flew to her mouth to cover up what she had already said.

Josh Cameron spluttered champagne as he pulled his glass quickly away from his mouth. "Canned lines?"

"I'm sorry. I shouldn't have said that."

"No, please, explain. I'm intrigued."

"It's just that, well, uh," Liv had dug herself into a big fat hole, and now she wished she could slide a door right over the top of it and never come back out. "When you say things like 'I feel so lucky to have met you' and 'To what's next,' it's maybe just a little, uh, cheesy?"

To Liv's relief, Josh Cameron started laughing. His dimples were deeper than she had ever seen them, and his eyes had started to tear up. *This* was not the response she had been expecting. "Olivia, that's priceless," he stammered, gasping for breath. "No one has *ever* said anything like that to me before."

"I'm really sorry. I shouldn't have said it. Your toast was very sweet." She couldn't believe she had just criticized Josh Cameron. *What is* wrong *with you, Liv?*

"No, please, don't be sorry. It's nice to hear the truth. Frankly, I get tired of the nonstop adoration from fans. Don't get me wrong, it's flattering to have people love you, but it's also nice to be brought back to earth from time to time." He smiled at her. "My apologies for the cheesy line. Mind if I try again?"

Liv shook her head, smiling meekly. She couldn't believe he wasn't furious she had just criticized him. This was too weird.

"To you, Olivia," Josh Cameron said, smiling widely. "The most refreshingly honest woman I have ever met."

Cheers to that, Liv thought, tipping her glass back. *Cheers to that.*

Yawning contentedly, Liv stretched her leg and wiggled her toes. She rolled over, eyes closed, and replayed the previous evening over and over in her head.

Things had gone a little fuzzy in the middle of dinner, but Liv could still remember most of her amazing night. She couldn't believe how incredibly sweet and sexy Josh Cameron was. After Liv had teased him for being cheesy, things had gotten much easier between them.

Liv thought back to the rest of their dinner conversation, and still couldn't believe that Josh Cameron, International Pop Star had opened up to her. "The thing is, sometimes you just want to be *normal*, you know?" he had said at one point during their meal. "That's why I appreciate your honesty so much, Olivia. You're not worried about what I'll think—you just say it like it is." He had smiled at her. "There's something unique about you—and I don't want that to sound like a line." Liv flushed as she remembered the way his eyes had lingered on hers.

Her memory of the rest of their meal was a bit of a blur, but she clearly remembered their dessert (some sort of gooey chocolate volcano) out on the balcony. The fresh air had revived her.

Liv had swaggered onto the balcony and moved to one of the glass walls to steady herself. She remembered leaning against the wall for support, and then strong hands circling around her waist like a safety net.

"Olivia," Josh Cameron had sighed, moving toward her. "I've had an amazing evening." His right hand had tightened around her waist as his left pushed a stray curl from her face. Liv congratulated herself on doing a quick tongue-check for food lodged between her teeth. She hadn't *expected* him to kiss her, but she wanted to be ready, just in case.

She could still feel the moment his lips first touched hers. Gently, cautiously at first, then expertly pressing into her more urgently. He delicately let his hand run through the length of her hair, then wrapped his soft hand around the back of her neck. He leaned back slightly to study her face in the moonlight as his thumb lazily traced a line across her jaw. Cupping her chin in his hand, he tilted her face upward gently before kissing her chin, each of her cheeks, and . . . finally . . . settling on her lips again.

She relived that kiss several more times before slowly opening her eyes. Yawning, Liv scanned the room, squinting to see her alarm clock. It was still dark, so she figured she had a few more hours to sleep, but wanted to make sure. As she searched in the dark for her clock, she suddenly became very aware that she was not alone. And she was very much not asleep on her couch-bed.

Where am I? Freaked out, Liv bolted upright and looked around. Her mind frantically raced through the rest of the previous night's date, desperately searching for an ending. *Oh no,* she thought, horrified. *Oh no. There was no ending. I don't remember an ending! I kissed him and then . . .* Nothing. Her memory was refusing to go beyond that kiss.

Racking her brain for details, the rest of the evening suddenly started trickling back into focus. After their balcony kiss, Josh Cameron had escorted Liv back inside the suite and they had settled into the corner of the couch. He had been talking about his ski trip to the Alps, and then . . . *Noooooo! I fell asleep!*

Liv squeezed her eyes shut, willing herself back in time. When she opened them, she hadn't moved. She realized she was sprawled out on the couch in the corner of Josh Cameron's hotel suite, covered in a fur blanket. She hadn't moved from the night before—even her shoes were still securely attached to her feet. She was feeling more than a little sheepish about her present situation. *How long have I been here?*

Looking across the room, Liv could see the outline of Skinny Guy, who was seated on a low footstool, his chin in his hands, watching her. When he saw that she was awake, he stood abruptly and moved toward her. "Mr. Cameron has retired for the evening," he explained briefly, helping Liv to her feet. "He has asked that I arrange for a car to take you home. He felt it best that you sleep here for a while, considering."

Considering what?! Liv wondered, suddenly nervous about what she had done or said. *How much did I drink?* She scolded herself for getting so out of hand. *I will never drink again. . . .*

"I took the liberty of ordering you a sandwich. Please feel free to bring it along for your ride home." Skinny Guy held a small pouch in her direction and made his way to the door. "Come along. Quickly."

Liv followed as Skinny Guy bustled down the hallway and led her into a dark, narrow elevator. She peeked into the sandwich pouch as the elevator descended, and groaned as her stomach protested. She had definitely had too much champagne if the sight of plain old ham and cheese was causing her stomach to curl.

Poking around inside the sandwich pouch, Liv found a small note next to the wrapped sandwich. "Olivia," it read, "Thank you for an incredible evening. I can't wait to see you again. Soon. Fondly, Josh Cameron." Liv smiled. He still had a way to go before he lost all of his cheesiness ("fondly" was just the tiniest bit old-fashioned), but at least he was sweet. She smiled as she reread his words. Soon, she thought, happily.

When the elevator reached the ground floor, Skinny Guy led Liv through the nearly deserted lobby. As they made their way past the frosted glass doors of the swanky hotel bar, though, she heard laughter and the clinking of glasses coming from within. The doors had whooshed open to welcome a stunning couple into the late-night gathering.

Liv craned her neck to try to get a glimpse of the inner reaches of the bar as Skinny Guy hurried her through the lobby. For a split second her heart caught in her throat—was that Josh Cameron on the other side of the bar's sliding doors? *Nah,* she thought, *impossible. Skinny Guy said he "retired for the evening"—and he wouldn't have left me in his room alone to go out.* Shrugging it off as her own overactive imagination, Liv smiled. *One amazing kiss, and I'm already paranoid,* she thought, giggling to herself.

Stifling a yawn, Liv made her way out of the lobby. With a sigh, she slid into the limo waiting outside the hotel—her limo!—and bit into her sandwich as the car sped her toward home.

Afternoon Delight

"Monet's inspiration for this piece . . ." *Blah, blah, blah-ba-di-blah.* Liv plopped down on one of the hard, backless benches in room thirty-four of the National Gallery and stared up at the famous Monet above her. She was only vaguely listening to the description. Her self-guided tour headphones had given her a headache, not to mention the fact that they had squished her ears flat and left one side of her hair panked tightly against her head.

When Liv had gotten up that morning, the weather was dreary and drizzly. After dragging herself out of bed and into the shower, Liv had returned to the living room and discovered that Rebecca's mood apparently matched the weather—she had settled herself in front of her sun lamp with a stack of fashion magazines, her iPod Nano, and a sneer. Hell Dog was by her side, snuggled tightly into Liv's blanket, soaking up the bright faux sunshine.

So Liv decided to get out of the apartment and do some London exploring. First stop: the National Gallery. Truth be told, Liv didn't really like museums all that much. In theory, she loved art—in reality, it got old really quickly.

So now, an hour after arriving, she was bored and weary—and hadn't yet made it out of the nineteenth-century wing. Leaning back on the bench, Liv turned the volume down on her headphones and focused on the crowd. This, she realized, was her favorite part of the museum. So many people from so many places. People who had seen so much more of the world than she had. She loved listening to the different languages, seeing their faces, studying their body language.

After a few minutes of people watching, Liv stood up and headed for the front hall. The rest of the museum would have to wait—she was ready to explore the city, and old art was getting her nowhere fast.

Breezing down the main stairs of the gallery, Liv plucked her visitor's tag off her T-shirt, returned her headphones, and slung her bag over her shoulder. She pushed the front door open and made her way out toward the lions in Trafalgar Square. The sun had burned through the clouds while she was in the museum, and the rain had cleared. It was a beautiful day.

"Liv!" Hearing her name, Liv turned back toward the gallery. A few steps behind her Colin was standing with his arm raised in a slight wave. "Sorry," he said breathlessly, "I thought that was you."

Liv's stomach flipped nervously. She was surprised to see Colin. And even more surprised he had stopped her—they hadn't spent much time together since he had started dating Rebecca. And at work he was always so distant and busy. "Hey, Colin. Were you at the gallery?"

"I was just on my way in—this is one of my favorite places in London. They make a fantastic cup of tea, and it's free admission." Colin shrugged. "But you look like you're off, then. See you at work tomorrow, yeah?"

Liv considered her options. She could walk away and spend the day alone, living out a solo adventure in London. Or she could be bold and invite herself to join Colin for a cup of tea. It certainly couldn't hurt to try to be friends. "Do you mind if I join you?"

Colin looked surprised, but—Liv noted happily—pleased. "Of course."

They walked up the steps of the museum together in silence. Liv didn't know what to say, but she felt compelled to fill the silence with unnecessary commentary. While Colin guided her through the halls to the museum café, she asked him endless questions about his flat, afternoon tea, and what it was like to grow up in Stratford-upon-Avon.

By the time they finally settled into a small table in the corner of the café, Liv had exhausted all of her generic questions and was almost out of things to say. Colin had barely uttered a word.

"Can I ask you something?" Liv silently vowed that this would be her last question. She *had* to stop talking.

"Isn't it a bit late to ask me that?" Colin smiled. *Aha,* Liv thought. *So he has noticed my endless chatter.*

"Sorry," Liv said, embarrassed. "I tend to talk a lot. I've never been very good with silence. It makes me uncomfortable."

"Yeah, I noticed," Colin said, immediately looking like he regretted being so honest. Liv laughed, noticing his embarrassment. "But it's a good thing," Colin said, by way of apology. "I tend to clam up around new people. Or I scare people off with my sarcasm. Go ahead—ask me anything."

"I sort of get the impression that you kind of avoid me at work." Liv could *not* believe she had just said that. But she was desperate to know what she had done to offend him.

"You do?" Colin furrowed his brow. "Sorry about that. I guess I've been a bit distracted. Andrew Stone is literally around every corner, and he doesn't like to see me not working. Rebecca has been stopping by my desk a lot lately, and he's sort of scolded me for—how does he put it?—'wasting his time.' So I try to stay focused, yeah?"

"Oh. Right." Now Liv felt bad. She should have figured Rebecca had something to do with his weird behavior. "It was rude of me to ask you that. I don't have a very good filter—really, pretty much everything that goes through my head comes out my mouth. I guess it's just a curse of being an only child. You can say whatever you want, and no one is there to hear you. So you just keep talking."

Colin laughed. "Don't worry about it. I like honesty—it's refreshing. My family tends to bottle up most of our issues and pretend all's well. So I like when people can express themselves. It's a nice change."

"Do you have a big family?"

"There you go with the questions again," Colin teased. "Kidding. I have two little sisters. So it's a pretty big family, yeah. You?"

"It's just me and my dad." Liv paused. There was something about Colin that made her feel safe. She *wanted* to tell him things. "My mom died in a car accident when I was little."

"I'm sorry," Colin said quietly. He paused, waiting for Liv to continue.

"It's okay. She was English. From London. So that's a big part of why I'm here. I'm trying to figure out what her life might have been like. Being here makes me feel so much closer to her." She paused, sipping her tea.

"Have you met anyone from your mom's family?"

"She was an only child, and her parents died before she did. I didn't know my grandparents at all. So there isn't really anyone left." Liv shrugged. "It's enough for me to soak up a little of her culture. I just want to feel like I've lived a part of her life. *Lived London*, you know?"

"That makes sense." Colin folded his napkin and set it on the table. "Well then, that's settled." Liv looked at him curiously. "I think it's time for us to get out and explore. Live some of the London life. Have you walked along the Thames yet? Visited Big Ben? Westminster Abbey? Buckingham Palace?"

Liv shook her head. She had done very little besides sit at her tollbooth and fetch Brown cups of watery coffee.

"Then I'll be your guide. We have a lot to see." He came around behind her and pulled her chair away from the table. Liv stood and followed as Colin guided her out of the museum, across Trafalgar Square, and down the Mall toward Buckingham Palace.

Hours later, after darkness had fallen and they stood together in the grainy light illuminating the turnstiles in the Charing Cross tube station, Liv was at a loss for words for the first time all day. "Colin, thank you," she finally said.

He smiled. "It was my pleasure. Have you had a good day?"

Liv and Colin had spent the afternoon chatting and laughing as they walked through St. James's Park and around Buckingham Palace, before eventually turning and going back toward Westminster Abbey and the River Thames. Colin led Liv past Big Ben and the Houses of Parliament, stopping only briefly for a second cup of tea in a small shop off Parliament Square. They had walked for hours, but Liv had hardly noticed.

"Amazing." Liv glanced at him. "I hope we can do it again sometime?"

"Me too." With that, he raised his hand in a little salute. "I hope you liked the tea at the museum. It really was the perfect cup, yeah?" Laughing, she waved as Colin backed out of the station, and then she turned and went down the escalator and toward home.

"I was starting to get worried about you," Anna greeted Liv from her position on the couch. "You've been gone all day."

"I ran into Colin outside the National Gallery," Liv said, throwing her bag into a heap in the corner of the living room. "We spent the day wandering around London."

"Sounds scandalous," Anna said, sitting up.

"It's not like that!" Liv insisted, swatting Anna as she settled into position on the couch. "But I think we can be friends." As she said it, Liv realized it was true. She had never actually pursued a friendship with a guy, and that afternoon had helped her realize how much fun it could be. She felt absolutely no pressure around Colin. She could be herself, and didn't have to worry about flirting or trying to figure out what to say so she didn't sound foolish. It was so easy and comfortable—it was actually a relief that he was taken, so she didn't have to worry about impressing him.

"Liv, seriously. Friends? He's hot. Maybe he's into you." Anna tucked her legs into a pretzel and fixed Liv with a stern stare.

Liv giggled and sat down next to her roommate. "Seriously. Friends. Yes, he's hot, but it's not like that. At all. I felt completely comfortable around him, and I don't want to ruin that by even thinking about hooking up with him. And hello—" Liv gestured down the hall and lowered her voice. "Rebecca. Though I did completely forget to ask him what's going on with them. He only mentioned her once, and I guess I wasn't so keen on bringing it up a second time."

Anna didn't look convinced. "Is this about Josh Cameron?" She frowned. Anna had been cautiously optimistic about Liv's date the night before. She said she couldn't help but feel suspicious of celebrities, and "needed to see what Josh Cameron's next move would be" before she would let Liv get too hopeful.

"No. And yes. Come on, Anna—you have to admit that things are going really well with Josh Cameron. I wouldn't say we're a 'couple,' but there's definitely hope, right?"

Anna nodded and grinned. "It's looking good."

"Trust me," Liv said. "I think Colin and I will be friends. But that's it. I'm not getting in her"—Liv gestured toward Rebecca's room—"way. Colin is clearly taken, so no matter what might have been, I'm not going there. Get it?"

"Got it."

"Good."

Sweet Dreams (Are Made of This)

Though she had meant it when she'd said it, Liv was finding it impossible to stick to her vow. She'd sworn she wasn't even the tiniest bit interested in Colin, but throughout the next week, Liv couldn't stop thinking about their weekend adventure.

She would recall funny stories Colin had told her about Andrew Stone as she filled Simon Brown's cup in the coffee room. She would catch herself smiling about how he always said "yeah?" like he was asking a question at the end of almost every sentence. And as she walked from the office to the tube every night, her mind flashed back to the way his eyes shone in the light of the Charing Cross tube station.

What she found most perplexing was the fact that she was obsessing about her totally normal afternoon strolling around London with Colin, but had spent almost no time dwelling on her steamy and fabulously chic dinner with Josh Cameron. *What's wrong with you, Liv?* She didn't like the tricks her emotions were playing on her. *You made out with the world's most coveted celebrity, and you're obsessing about some* random *guy from Stratford-upon-Avon? Some English dude who is crazy enough to go out with your psycho roommate?*

Liv could only hope this Colin nonsense was her mind's way of trying to prevent her from obsessing about Josh Cameron. Luckily, stuffing Colin to the back of her mind became much easier after she caught a glimpse of his hand on Rebecca's back as they wandered down the Music Mix hallway deep in conversation one afternoon—*yuck!* So she focused her energy on willing Josh Cameron to call and ask her out again.

Simon Brown was particularly gruff and surly all week, so Liv didn't have too much time at the office to focus on anything but his bizarre needs. Brown had developed an unexpected addiction to Nicorette—the stop-smoking gum—and had begun to send Liv out to fetch three or four or twenty packs most afternoons. The gum didn't seem to do much for Brown, since he still went through at least two packs of cigarettes a day—usually lighting up as he stuffed a fresh piece of Nicorette into his mouth. This dual habit resulted in breath that smelled like a public bathroom, so Liv was relieved that she rarely needed to get close enough to be hit with the full effect.

On her way back into the Music Mix building one evening, her arms loaded with packs of Nicorette and Dunhill cigarettes, Liv spotted Anna pushing her way out of the revolving door. Anna quickly rushed over to relieve Liv of some of her packages. "Hey," Liv said, breathless. "Thanks. You going home?"

"Yeah," Anna said quietly. "Rough day."

Liv tilted her head, confused. Anna didn't have a lot of rough days—her Music Mix assignment suited her perfectly, and her whole department loved her. So most days, Anna came home glowing with happiness. "What's up?"

"Nothing major. It's nothing, really." Anna looked up defiantly and smiled.

"Hmm," Liv responded, studying Anna

carefully. She didn't believe that for a second. "Are you sure?"

Anna smiled weakly. "I promise."

"You know what? I think I can get out of here—let me just run this stuff up to Brown and grab my bag. We can go home together." Liv always ended up riding the tube home alone, since she usually worked hours later than any of the other interns. But she wasn't going to let Anna go home alone—to Rebecca—when she seemed so upset.

"Really? You can leave at . . . ," Anna said sarcastically, glancing at her watch, ". . . seven thirty?"

"Crazy, isn't it? Yeah, just hang out here for a sec and I'll be right back. Promise you'll wait?"

Anna nodded, so Liv gathered up all her packages and made her way up the escalators to deliver Brown's goods. Luckily, Brown was engrossed in watching an episode of *Footballers' Wives* and just grunted when Liv dropped the bags on his desk and announced that she was leaving. So she breezed back down the hall and out the door to her waiting roommate.

Anna filled their walk to the tube with superficial stories of what had happened at the office that day. Liv listened and nodded, but couldn't help wondering what was going on. Anna was clearly trying to keep talking to prevent Liv from asking any more questions. Finally Liv couldn't stand it anymore and just blurted out, "If there's something going on—if there's anyone whose butt needs kicking—you know I'm your girl, right?"

Anna laughed.

"I'm serious," Liv continued. "I don't want to force you to tell me what's going on, but I'm not pretending that everything's dandy. You're clearly avoiding something. . . ."

They had reached the tube station and were riding down the escalator to the tracks. Liv and Anna both pressed to the right side of the escalator, allowing hustling Londoners to walk past them on the left. Liv had quickly learned that this was an unspoken rule of the tube that people were *very* serious about. . . . Never stand on the left side of the escalator.

Anna turned to face Liv as they descended underground. She explained, "Everything's fine. Things are just stressful with my parents right now. But I really don't want to get into it."

"Your mom? Are there new developments?"

"No, same old stuff. She's just really been on me lately, and it's sort of sucking the fun out of this summer. She hasn't even asked me how the internship is going—we just avoid talking about it. She only calls to tell me what she's buying for my dorm room next year."

"So she hasn't relented at all, huh?"

"It's gotten worse. And the more she talks about *my* plans for school, the more I'm convinced I'm not ready to go yet. I'm loving this job so much, and know that if I just had one year to pursue this, I would be so much happier with the next ten years of my life being committed to Oxford and med school or whatever." Anna sighed as they boarded their train.

Liv began to respond, but Anna cut her off. "Can we talk about something else? Make me laugh," Anna begged. "I want to take my mind off this."

Realizing she meant it, Liv thought for a second before pulling her iPod out of her bag. She scrolled through the song list, then stuck one earbud in Anna's ear, and the other in her own. "Music therapy," she explained, pressing play on the dial. "If the sight of me gettin' down in the tube doesn't make you laugh, nothing will."

As ABBA sang out, *"You can dance, you can jive, having the time of your life . . ."* Liv wiggled her butt and waved her arms in the air. Passengers in the train looked up from their newspapers to stare at her. Anna started to laugh, and a flush of red crept up her cheeks.

"Okay, okay! Stop—this is mortifying." Anna continued to laugh as Liv drew even more stares.

"Did I take your mind off it?" Liv whispered as she continued to shimmy more subtly in time to the music. Anna nodded. "Then it was worth it." The doors opened at their stop, and Liv and Anna hustled out, still joined at the ear by the iPod.

The next morning when Liv walked into the Music Mix lobby, Gloria stood up from her desk and whispered, "Look out . . . he's on the hunt."

Liv paused. "Brown?"

"Who else?" Gloria asked, nodding. "He's in rare form today—be prepared."

With a groan, Liv pressed through the door leading out of the lobby and braced herself for a fun day. As she passed Brown's open door, he shouted "Oy!" and waved her over.

"Good morning," she said, trying to start their conversation out on the right foot.

Brown just stared at her and launched into a list of instructions. "This will need to go," he said, gesturing toward two large boxes in the corner of his office, "as will this. I've arranged for a courier to pick you up and take you there. Don't irritate me with nonsensical questions. Go, Girl!"

Right-o, Liv thought, more confused than ever. *You got it.* She clumsily gathered the two enormous boxes in the corner of Brown's office into her arms and made her way back out to the main lobby. Setting the boxes on the corner of the reception desk, Liv just looked at Gloria and broke out laughing.

"Here's what I figure," Gloria said, without Liv's needing to ask. "The Josh Cameron concert is coming up. They're in the final prep stages, and Brown is starting to freak out. I'm guessing the car service that just called from downstairs is here to pick you and those boxes up and deliver you to the stadium. Make sense?"

"I'd say that's as good a guess as any. I

suppose it can't hurt to get in the car and see where it takes me." She thanked Gloria, hoisted the boxes into her arms again, and made her way down the escalator. Outside, a driver was waiting next to a black car. Liv moved toward the backseat, and the driver whisked the door open for her. *So far, so good,* she thought.

Twenty minutes later Liv's car stopped outside the service entrance to a huge stadium. She made her way inside and wandered around aimlessly for a few minutes before running into Rebecca, who was bustling through the hallway with a clipboard and walkie-talkie, shouting things to stagehands and mechanics. When she spotted Liv, Rebecca came gliding over.

"Oh, Li-uhv, are those the dog beds?"

Liv just grunted. She had no idea what was in the boxes, but really hoped that a private car hadn't been hired to deliver a bunch of dog beds to the stadium. "No clue," she responded. "I was just told to bring these boxes here." Liv set down her packages and opened up one of the boxes. *You've got to be kidding me,* she mused. *Rebecca was right.*

Rebecca smiled smugly and directed Liv to one of the rooms behind the stage. "Just unpack the beds and make it nice and comfy in there, won't you? We want to make sure all our special guests are taken care of during the concert. Thanks, sweetie."

Liv spent the next hour and a half unpacking and fluffing dog beds in a small, rectangular room down the hall from the stage. She wasn't sure why she was preparing this little doggie hotel, but she had come to realize that her summer job entailed doing as she was told, and understanding later.

Liv finished quickly and decided to take a peek around the stadium—she had heard so much about the concert from Rebecca, but hadn't gotten to check things out for herself. Now that she was maybe-dating the star of the show, she felt like she deserved a little peek.

She made her way down the hall toward the stage, pulling aside the curtain that blocked off the backstage area. Liv's breath caught in her throat when she spotted Josh Cameron's familiar curls at the back of the stage. She hadn't really thought about how she would respond the next time she saw him, but now that he was so close she was suddenly panicked at the thought of seeing him again. *He kissed me, he kissed me, he kissed me*—that was all she could think about as she stepped onstage and walked toward Josh Cameron.

As she approached, he turned to her, his face a blank slate. He stared at her for a few seconds before a smile spread across his face. "Excuse me," he said, motioning to the sound engineer he had been talking to. "Olivia."

"Hey," she said, still nervous. "Hi." She grinned awkwardly. "How are you?"

Josh Cameron moved toward her, his eyes penetrating hers. "I hope you made it home safely on Friday."

"Oh! Yeah, fine. No problems. Thanks for the sandwich."

He looked confused. "Oh," he said. "Right. So tell me, Olivia. To what do I owe this surprise?"

"You mean, why am I here? I brought the dog beds." *That's great, Liv. Reeeeeally charming.*

"Right. The dog beds." Josh Cameron was smirking at her. "I don't suppose you have some time before you have to get back?"

Liv was definitely not in a hurry to get back to Brown, and she figured her task had taken less time than expected. "Sure, I'm free. Why?"

"I was just on my way to the Berkeley Hotel for tea. Care to join me?"

Forty-five minutes later Liv was still waiting on a plastic folding chair by the stage door. She had happily agreed to tea, and he had told her he would be "just a mo'." Many, many mo's later, she was starting to get impatient. She was also a little nervous about how long she'd been gone from the office. Finally, almost an hour later, the pop star emerged from the stage area. He approached Liv and offered her a hand, making no comment about the time that had passed.

But the wait was worth it. When Josh Cameron's limo delivered them to the door of the Berkeley Hotel, they were quickly ushered inside to a private table tucked into a corner. Liv wasn't offered a menu, but their table was almost instantly filled with towering platters of pastries, cookies, and sandwiches, steaming pots of tea, and cucumber wedges. The pastries and cookies were stunning, one-of-a-kind masterpieces. Josh Cameron watched her with an amused expression as she bit into a deep chocolate cookie with white trim.

"You know," he said, "that cookie was inspired by a classic Chanel dress."

"Am I supposed to eat it?" Liv asked, only half-joking.

Josh Cameron laughed. "Of course. But each of these cookies takes hours to design. That's what makes this place so inspired." Liv nodded, self-consciously nibbling at the cookie.

At the next table over, Liv could hear two ladies gushing about the service and, of all things, the table linens. Then one of them gasped and too-loudly whispered, "High tea at this hotel has more than a monthlong waiting list."

Liv giggled and looked across her table at Josh Cameron, who raised an eyebrow and smirked. "One of the benefits of dating a celebrity, wouldn't you say?"

Liv nodded, her cheeks flushing at what he had just said—Josh Cameron had defined them as "dating"! Giddy with the knowledge that she was officially dating the world's most eligible bachelor, Liv floated through the rest of the afternoon.

Yet for some strange reason, her dream-world didn't feel quite as perfect as she had always envisioned.

Girls Just Want to Have Fun

At six o'clock on Friday morning, Liv was jolted awake by a loud, tinny rendition of the Black Eyed Peas' "My Humps." Moaning, she rolled over on her couch-bed and covered her head with a pillow, cursing herself for changing Anna's ring tone from *Für Elise*. As she lay there, trying to muffle the sound of Anna's cell phone, she snuck a peek at her clock—*it's really early,* she mused sleepily. *What could be this important?*

She could hear Anna's door open, and she felt the thumping of her roommate running for her phone. Anna snapped open the phone in the kitchen and murmured a quiet "Mama" into the phone. *It's her mom?* Liv wondered, starting to worry. *Whose mom calls at six in the morning?!*

Anna spoke quickly and quietly in Swedish. Liv listened to her lilting voice, noticing a tense, agitated tone. There was a brief pause, and then Liv heard Anna flip the phone closed. Her roommate stood in the kitchen for a few minutes, while Liv pretended to be asleep. She wanted to sit up and ask what was going on, but she knew that Anna would let her know if and when she was ready to talk.

"Everything okay?" Liv asked sleepily. She had minded her own business for less than thirty seconds, and she just couldn't help it—Liv *had* to know that Anna was okay.

"Yeah," Anna said, lying down beside Liv on the couch-bed and flopping her head back into a pillow. "That was my mom." Long silence. "She's coming to London tomorrow morning. Apparently we 'need to talk.' And I guess it's an in-person conversation. She's flying in from Stockholm on the first flight in the morning. She'll be here by eight."

Liv breathed out. "Are you okay with that?"

"I guess I have to be, don't I?" Anna said

bitterly. "She hasn't exactly given me a whole lot of options."

"Any idea what inspired this visit *now*?"

Anna groaned. "I have a pretty good idea."

Liv rolled onto her side, facing her friend. "Do you want to tell me?"

"I don't know why I haven't told you this yet," Anna said sheepishly. "I guess I didn't really want to say it out loud, because it makes it more real." She exhaled. "I turned down every university I was accepted to for the fall. I sent letters out earlier this week, and I guess they already got them and have started calling my house to find out why I'm declining their offers.

"I know I made the right decision," Anna continued, closing her eyes. "But I still need to justify that to my mom. I know I'll go to university sometime—I'm just not ready right now. I need to figure out what I want to do with my life first. I just need a year or two to try things and figure out what fits, you know? And if there's the tiniest chance I could get a job at Music Mix, I *need* to try."

"So your mom is coming to try to change your mind?"

"I guess," Anna said, flopping her hands

at her sides. "It's not going to work, so it seems like sort of a useless trip. It's not like I just—*poof!*—made the decision. . . . There was some thought involved," she continued bitterly. "But I guess we need to get it out into the open. I couldn't have really hidden the decision from her. She would have found out eventually, so this conversation is probably inevitable."

"Probably," Liv mused. "If it helps, I think you made the right decision."

Anna sat up suddenly, swinging her legs off the side of Liv's bed. "Thanks. Can we go get a yummy breakfast before work to clear my head?"

"Do you want me to make you breakfast?" Liv offered, secretly hoping Anna would say no. She could cook pancakes from a box and that was just about it. A scone from a café sounded much more appealing.

"Liv, get real. I've seen you cook. That's almost more of a punishment than my mom's visit." Anna grinned. "Move it. If we hurry, we'll escape before Rebecca even wakes up."

An hour later Anna and Liv had settled into a window seat at Tully's, which had become Liv's favorite coffee shop. The staff had become friendly with Liv, thanks to all the lattes and cappuccinos she fetched for *Hits Parade* celebrities and their assistants.

When they had arrived a few minutes after seven, they were given a pot of tea and scones with clotted cream—on the house. Liv grinned through a mouthful of scone and said, "Simon Brown has his benefits, doesn't he? There's nothing like free breakfast to make all those coffee runs worth it. Feel better?"

Anna nodded. "Much."

As she slurped her tea, Liv asked, "Do you want to talk about your strategy for tomorrow morning?" She had been a little hesitant to remind Anna about her mom's visit, but Anna still seemed distracted.

"Nah, I'm good. I promise. Thank you for asking, though—and talking me through it this morning." Anna waved her hand dismissively and set her face in a playfully stern scowl. "Here's what I want. . . . I want to sit here and eat until I'm sick, and then spend the night dancing it off. Tonight's club night, remember?"

"That's tonight?" Liv asked. With all the excitement of the past week, Liv had sort of forgotten that all the interns were going out that night. Anna and Francesco had been planning it for weeks. Apparently, the wardrobe department was way more into work-life balance than Simon Brown was—Anna's boss had even forced her to take one afternoon off to go check out a potential club for their intern outing. "I totally forgot. Wow, Anna, I'm losing my mind."

Anna smiled for the first time all morning. "You're distracted. But I still love you for helping me with this mom stuff. Now, no more serious talk. I'll deal with tomorrow, tomorrow. Tonight, we dance."

"Ah just don't know if I should wear my Jimmy Choos or my Manolos. Which of them makes me look more precious?" Liv and Anna were sitting in the living room, trying desperately not to laugh.

Rebecca had tried on no fewer than six outfits, each of which had a matching ensemble for My Rover. She had finally settled on a small pink dress and a silver clutch, outfitting My Rover in silver booties and a pink cape. Hell Dog was now scratching madly at the booties while Rebecca debated between five-inch peekaboo-toed stilettos and six-inch silver pumps.

"We have to leave," Anna said in reply, sending Rebecca over the edge.

Near tears, Rebecca looked at Liv with a look of desperation. "Ah just can't decide," she said, her lip quivering.

"The pumps," Liv said matter of factly, desperate to calm Rebecca down and get them out of the apartment on time. "Definitely the Manolo pumps. It totally coordinates your look with Rover."

"*My* Rover," Rebecca clarified, narrowing her eyes at Liv. "This precious darling's name is *My* Rover." Her tears had been replaced with a steely, stern voice. "The Jimmy Choos it is." She slipped on the heels, swept My Rover into her arms, and headed out the door.

Anna and Liv exchanged a look. "Perfect. Great choice, Rebecca," Liv yelled loudly after her. "You look perfect."

Thirty minutes later the three roommates emerged from the tube and made their way toward Runway, a swanky club that Anna promised Liv she would love. Anna had booked a table, and the other Music Mix interns were meeting them there.

When they walked in to the club, Liv could hardly believe it was real. The rectangular room was draped in deep red furs, and awash in understated white light glowing from within a long, fashion show–like catwalk that jutted out into the center of the room. Tables were arranged along the length of the runway, and frighteningly thin waitresses and waiters strutted up and down the length of the catwalk to deliver drinks.

Liv's mouth hung open, her face an expression of pure disbelief. Club owners went to such bizarre lengths to create a unique and glamorous atmosphere. Back in Ann Arbor, the high school gym outfitted for prom had always been considered exotic. Anna looked at Liv and burst out laughing.

Rebecca lifted one eyebrow and studied her nails. Clearly, this scene was very familiar to Rebecca—or she was playing the part very well.

As they walked toward the hostess, Anna shouted, "I picked this club because I heard it's pretty fabulous. Later they open the runway up to the crowd and you can vamp it up, supermodel-style. Sounds fun, doesn't it?"

Liv leaned in to Anna. "This is incredible. I assure you that there is no way I'll be walking that catwalk, but this is truly awesome. You picked a great place."

Anna took Liv's hand and led her toward

their table. Rebecca trailed a safe distance behind, trying to look like she wasn't with them. The group squeezed through the crowds lingering near the front of the club and moved toward the runway.

Liv spotted Francesco bounding up from a table right alongside the center of the runway. He ran over and gathered her and Anna into a tight hug, planting kisses on their cheeks. "Welcome, welcome!" he shouted, his Italian accent more pronounced than usual.

Francesco moved to the table and pulled chairs out for both of them. Rebecca crossed her arms as best she could (My Rover was tucked delicately under one arm) and cleared her throat. Colin stood up from his place at the table and offered his chair.

The table was packed with Music Mix interns, some of whom Liv knew only from their daily trips to the coffee machine. Others—like Katia, one of the other Americans, and Alex, from Russia—she had snuck into the Green Room for lunch a few times. Liv settled into her seat and looked up at the runway, soaking in every possible moment.

Realizing that all eyes were on her, Liv adjusted her jeans just slightly and steadied herself on Anna's heels. She inched forward in time to the music, trying desperately to sedate her nerves. She still didn't know exactly how she had gotten here.

In an effort to look confident, Liv wiggled her butt and curtsied, soliciting cheers and whistles from the crowded club. She held Anna's sweaty hand tightly by her side, clutching it like a life raft. Looking to her left, Liv could see all the Music Mix interns sitting at the table smiling and laughing, urging them on. Liv glanced at Anna, who was grinning ear to ear beside her. She winked at Liv as they took a step down the runway.

Before Liv had accepted Anna's dare to hop up on the catwalk, she made Anna promise to join her. Double humiliation felt much better than going it alone. The catwalk looked like it was a mile long, and they had only gone two steps. But it was too late to turn back now.

Liv steeled her nerves as she and Anna moved forward again. Suddenly the music (which had been some cheesy, uninspiring Rick Springfield song) changed, and the first notes of ABBA's "Dancing Queen" came flowing out of the speakers lining the runway.

"You can dance, you can jive, having the time of your life . . ."

Anna and Liv looked at each other as they recognized the familiar lyrics and burst out laughing.

"See that girl, watch that scene, dig in the Dancing Queen . . ."

"This is definitely becoming our theme song, isn't it?" Liv yelled in Anna's ear.

Anna nodded, grinning. "Feel better about doing this now?" she yelled back.

Putting all shame aside, the two strutted down the runway in unison and shimmied in time to the music. They knew they looked completely ridiculous, but they were having so much fun that it really didn't matter.

As they hammed it up on the runway, Liv caught a glimpse of Rebecca dancing next to Colin on the floor. In fact, when she looked around, everyone in the club was dancing. No one was laughing at them— instead, everyone looked like they were having an incredible time. When the last notes chimed out of the speakers, both Liv and Anna slid to their knees, arms raised, and struck a pose. Everyone in the club was cheering, and the Music Mix interns all ran to the end of the runway to help them off the platform.

"That was incredible!" Katia screamed.

"Hilarious," Francesco chimed in.

Liv and Anna looked at each other and cracked up. "I can't believe we just did that," Anna said, giggling and gasping to catch her breath.

Laughing, Liv responded, "You *said* you wanted to dance tonight. You rocked!"

The rest of the night went by in a blur. In no time they were being whisked out of the club and into a taxi home. Liv settled into the backseat and leaned against Anna. She smiled and closed her eyes as "Dancing Queen" ran through her head over and over—*You can dance, you can jive, having the time of your life . . .*

I am, Liv thought happily. *I am having the time of my life.*

Should I Stay or Should I Go?

As promised, Anna's mom arrived early the next morning, and her knock at the door startled Liv from a deep, contented sleep. Anna hustled out of her bedroom, dressed and ready. She hurried through an introduction while Liv sat snuggled up under her covers in her couch-bed. She had made a motion to stand up for a proper handshake, but Anna's mom insisted she stay in bed.

Anna hastily showed her mom around their apartment, and less than five minutes later, Anna declared they were leaving. She and Liv had decided during the previous night's taxi ride home that Anna should take her mom out shopping and for high tea at Selfridges to soften her up a bit.

Liv hoped everything would be okay—she couldn't imagine the pressure Anna must be feeling. The phone calls and arguments had really taken their toll on her. Liv hoped Anna and her mom could sort things out so Anna could enjoy the rest of her summer guilt-free.

Though she would never admit it to Anna, Liv did sort of envy her roommate's parents' involvement in her life. Liv's dad was incredible, but she sometimes wished he paid more attention to what she was doing. She wouldn't even mind if he got a little more angry when she screwed up. He was often so wrapped up in his photography that Liv sometimes wondered if he noticed she was growing up. She only had one year left at home before she went off to college.

But now that she'd seen Anna's situation, she was beginning to realize that her dad's lack of involvement in decisions about her life was probably just his way of letting her know he supported her. He never said it, but maybe his silence was his way of encouraging her to make her own choices. *Hmmm,* she thought. *Interesting trick.*

Pulling herself out of bed, Liv realized she had the whole day to herself. Rebecca was in the shower, and seemed to be getting ready to go out. So Liv happily lazed around the apartment—under the careful watch of Hell Dog—before deciding how best to spend the day.

She was still surviving almost exclusively on Green Room leftovers, and she felt like she deserved a tasty lunch at one of the neighborhood pubs. She could hole away in a dark corner and work on ideas for the VJ for a Day competition. Things had been so hectic at work that she and Anna had had almost no time to think about their audition. They still had a month before the competition, but Liv knew how crazy things were going to get around the office with the Josh Cameron concert coming up.

Around noon she wandered out into the rainy early afternoon and into a pub just a few blocks from her flat. She was instantly comforted by the warm, dark interior, and she spotted a small open table in the back corner. The cozy restaurant made her feel very literary and Shakespeare-esque—she hoped the environment would inspire great ideas for the audition.

As she passed through the dark room, Liv's stomach dropped. Sitting in one of the deep red booths along the side wall was a way-too-familiar blond head. *Rebecca,* she groaned inwardly.

Rebecca spotted Liv just as Liv was deciding whether she could make a quick getaway, or if she had to stop and say hello. She realized that running off wasn't the most adult thing to do, but she didn't know if she could handle spending her lunch with Rebecca. *Maybe I'll get lucky and Rebecca will be with someone,* Liv mused. *Maybe she doesn't want to see me any more than I want to see her.*

Just as quickly as she had hoped Rebecca wasn't alone, Liv took it back. Because Rebecca was very definitely having lunch with someone . . . and that someone was Colin. Sure, Liv had vowed that she and Colin were just friends—and she was dating Josh Cameron, International Superstar—but she still cringed when she saw them together.

"Oh," Liv blurted out. "Hi, Rebecca. Hi, Colin."

"Li-uhv," Rebecca purred coldly. "How marvelous to see you here." *Is she joking?* Liv thought, her stomach churning.

Colin shot Rebecca a look, and said quickly, "Liv, join us."

Now, Liv could think of *nothing* she would rather *not* do at that moment than join Rebecca and Colin for lunch. But she could see no escape.

"So, what are you guys up to today?" Liv asked, though she wasn't entirely sure she wanted to know the answer.

"We're just—," Colin began, but Rebecca quickly cut him off.

"Oh, Li-uhv, Colin is just so sweet," she said, leaning in conspiratorially toward Liv. "He's taking me all around London today, showing me all of the sights. Isn't that just the sweetest thing you've ever heard?" She beamed across the table at Colin as Liv willed herself not to puke.

Although she was being totally unreasonable, Liv just couldn't stop herself from feeling pangs of jealousy. For some dumb reason, she thought Colin's tour around London had been for her alone. She now realized just how silly that assumption was.

What's wrong with you, Liv? Did you think Colin might be interested in you even though he knows about you and Josh Cameron, and he's clearly dating Rebecca? Did you think he was going to wait around for you?

"Yeah," Liv said, after a moment's silence. "That's really sweet, Rebecca." She glanced at Colin, who was focusing on the table in front of him.

"Are you *alone* today, Liv?" Rebecca asked with a smirk. "Where's Josh Cameron?"

All right, Liv thought bitterly. *Is that question really necessary?* Out loud, she said, "Oh, I'm not sure. You know how it is— preparing for his concert and everything. He's a busy guy." *Lame, Liv. Totally lame.* Liv had tried to keep the details of her relationship quiet, but her close friends knew she was "hanging out" with an International Superstar. Rebecca, however, was convinced Liv was making it all up.

"Yeah, Ah definitely know how it is. The concert is going to be fab-u-lous, by the way," Rebecca said with an air of superiority. Liv thought she noticed Colin shoot Rebecca a weird look across the table, but she couldn't be sure.

After a moment of awkward silence, Colin spoke. "We should probably get going, yeah?"

"Right," Rebecca said cheerfully. "Big day. Liv, you should definitely try the shepherd's pie. Ah tried some of Colin's and it was absolutely dee-lish."

Liv muttered something and hastily said good-bye. As Colin and Rebecca headed for the door, she noticed Colin lean over and mutter something quietly to Rebecca.

Rebecca frowned, then turned to look back at Liv. She broke into a huge pageant grin and waved. Liv managed a thin smile, then slid further into the booth.

"Urghhhhhh."

Liv looked up from her book as the door slammed. "Didn't go so well?" she asked, as Anna threw herself onto the couch.

"You could say that," Anna said, clunking her head against the back of the couch.

Liv folded down the corner on her page and tossed her book on the floor. "Details, please. If you want to share."

"Yeah, I'll share. I think I need to." Anna stood up and went to the fridge. She returned a moment later with two glasses of black currant juice and a packet of biscuits. "Let's just say, she isn't happy with me."

"Did high tea help?" Liv asked, smiling.

"Uh-huh," Anna mumbled, tearing open the cookies. "That was a good idea—she totally loved it. But she's still *really* upset with me. She says I broke our agreement."

"Yikes."

"I mean, I did say if she gave me this summer, I'd get back on track this fall. But I agreed to that when I didn't think there was really a chance I would be putting off college for a few years. But, Liv, I just can't do it." Anna had tears welling up in her eyes. Liv set her glass on the floor and leaned forward to give her roommate a hug.

Anna continued. "I don't know what I am going to do. I *know* I'll go to school—there's even a good chance I'll apply to med school—and that's part of the reason I feel like I have to take a couple years to explore now."

"What did your mom say to all that?" Liv asked.

"It was the first time I'd ever really mentioned any of this to her, so I think it came as a surprise. She just assumed I wanted everything she wanted. But I want to work at Music Mix! Not forever, but for a little while. . . ." Anna smiled weakly.

"I know you do." Liv didn't really know what to say. So she just sat and waited for Anna to continue.

"I know it's unlikely that I'll get a job from Simon Brown at the end of the summer, but I need to try," Anna said resolutely. "And if that doesn't work out, then I'll figure something else out. It feels so good not to have a plan—I know that sounds silly, but my whole life has been completely planned out, and I love that it could be a blank slate for the next few years."

Liv nodded. Everything Anna was saying made complete sense. But she couldn't stop thinking that the situation Anna was dealing with was the complete opposite of the one she would be dealing with in a year. She'd gotten so little pressure, and had so few ideas of what she was going to do, that college seemed like the only option for her. She was looking forward to the structure.

Anna guzzled the rest of her juice. "You know, even though today was awful and painful and really, really unpleasant, I'm glad I had a chance to talk to her about it. I think that she might sort of get it. Even though she's upset, I'm sort of hoping that on some level she understands what I've been going through. It's possible she might ease up for a while. At least until application season comes around again," Anna broke off, laughing.

Liv was happy to see Anna's mood brightening. "So you think you guys are good now?"

"Not good. But maybe better. I understand where she's coming from, and she understands that I need to do what I'm going to do, and forcing me to do something else isn't going to accomplish much." Anna grinned. "Even though I'm stubborn, I'm not stupid. . . . She knows I'll make the 'right' choices"—she made little quotes in the air—"eventually."

"You will *definitely* make the right choices," Liv said. "You have up until now, so I don't think there's much risk of that."

Anna stood up and turned on some music. "Now we just need to focus on getting me a job at Music Mix so I'm not homeless and penniless at the end of the summer," she laughed. "How was your day, dear?"

Liv groaned. "Not as terrible as yours, but definitely not good."

"Why?" Anna asked. "What happened?"

Liv quickly told Anna about her run-in with Colin and Rebecca. "It was just so awkward," she finished.

"You are totally into him," Anna said simply.

"What? No."

"I don't know—that's what it sounds like to me."

"That's crazy." Liv shook her head. "What about Josh Cameron? And what about the fact that Colin is dating *Rebecca*? There's something really wrong with him if he's attracted to her."

"Mmm-hmm." Anna grinned. As Liv reached over to swat her roommate with a pillow, the door to their apartment flew open and Rebecca floated in.

"Hi, girls," she said, winking. The look on Rebecca's face told Liv everything she needed to know. And it was then—Josh Cameron and Rebecca aside—that Liv realized Anna may have been more than a little bit right.

I Think We're Alone Now

The next week flew by.

Liv hadn't heard anything from Josh Cameron since their tea at the Berkeley Hotel. She hadn't *really* noticed over the weekend, but as soon as she was at work on Monday, she became obsessed. She was, of course, hoping he might call or pop by her tollbooth at Music Mix. She held on to that hope throughout Monday and into Tuesday morning, eventually suffering a mild case of whiplash from looking up quickly every time someone came near her desk.

On Tuesday afternoon she convinced herself that this sort of behavior was normal for a pop star, and obviously she couldn't expect him to drop everything to make time for her.

By Wednesday she had rediscussed the situation with Anna so many times that Liv was starting to suspect Anna was avoiding her.

On Thursday she began to question whether she had totally misinterpreted their relationship.

By Friday, however, she was mad. Still no call.

Liv would never receive the Lifetime Achievement Award for Dating, but she did know that this sort of behavior was strange, to say the least. And something deep down was telling her that she should run as fast as possible the other way, pop star or not—this guy was not worth waiting for.

Finally released from the office at five o'clock on Friday with a hearty "Go, Girl!" Liv decided to drink away her Josh Cameron paranoia with a large café mocha and a side of treacle pudding at Tully's. Several minutes later she settled into a window table, shrugged off her sweater, and dug into her dessert.

She pulled out a notebook, hoping the caffeine kick would inspire some great ideas for the VJ for a Day audition. Liv had been thinking about the competition almost constantly, but had still come up with a grand total of zero good ideas.

Liv and Anna swore they would spend every night the next week planning. They were desperate to win, but they knew they had very little chance if they didn't get to work soon.

As she stuck her pen in her mouth, accidentally suctioning the cap to her tongue, Liv felt someone brush up behind her. Turning, Liv noticed Colin sitting down at the table behind her.

"Hey," she said, lifting an arm to wave.

"Hello you. All right?" Liv nodded and smiled. She loved how the English simply said "All right?" rather than "Are you all right?" or "How are you?" It just seemed so much simpler.

"Did you just get off work?" Liv closed her notebook and unsuctioned the pen cap from her tongue. A little raised bump had been left in its place.

"Long day, yeah? Mind if I join you?"

"For sure." Liv reached her leg out and pulled a spare chair to her table. "Have a seat."

"Ta." *Aha,* Liv thought, *another good Britishism—"ta."* The simple, short version of "thanks." She sometimes thought British English could be more difficult to follow than a foreign language. "So," Colin continued. "What are you working on?" He motioned to her notebook.

Liv shrugged. "Nothing, really. I was hoping to get started on our VJ for a Day audition stuff." She took a sip of her drink. "Anna and I are working on it together, but we're sort of having a hard time figuring out what to do."

"Well, don't they always say you're supposed to play to your strengths?" Colin said, sounding like Liv's high school guidance counselor. "What do you like? What are you passionate about?"

Liv considered Colin's question. "Lucky Charms. I really like Lucky Charms cereal. But you can't get it in England."

"Lucky Charms. Interesting." Colin nodded seriously. "Could be a good angle. But what I meant was, what are your music passions? You know, what kind of music do you like?"

"Ohhhh." Liv grinned. "Okay . . . honest answer, or appropriate for Music Mix answer?"

Colin laughed. "Honest answer."

"I love the seventies and eighties. I

grew up listening to ABBA, The Bangles, Blondie, U2, stuff like that. And I know the lyrics to every single Eagles song. No joke."

"Impressive," Colin said, nodding. "Maybe you should just do an Eagles singalong? Showcase your unique talent," Colin suggested.

"I'm sure that would go over well," Liv said, laughing. "Thanks for the help. We'll figure it out eventually, I'm sure." She grabbed her bag and stuffed her notebook into it. "Did you know," she asked, smiling, "that today is the Fourth of July? If I were home, I would be getting ready to go to a picnic at the lake to celebrate."

"Obviously," Colin cut in, "here in London we won't be celebrating America's Independence from England."

"Obviously," Liv agreed.

"Though, the English are glad to be rid of you." Colin smirked. "Happy Independence!"

"Funny," Liv said, smiling. She felt so relaxed around him—his humor was weird, but it somehow it seemed to match hers perfectly. "Now, just because it's not a holiday here doesn't mean we have to mope around like it's some regular day. I think we should celebrate something. Say, for example, our independence from Music Mix—good-bye, Simon Brown and Andrew Stone. If only for the weekend."

"I'm up for it," Colin said, downing the rest of his Ribena juice box. "What do you have in mind?"

"I'm thinking hot dogs, sodas, blockbuster movie—your typical Fourth of July stuff." She grinned. "Some traditions are hard to break. Sound good?"

"Delicious. Very American." Colin nodded. "However . . . seeing as this is England, how would you feel about doing something a little more British?"

"Sure," Liv said, shrugging. "I'm up for anything."

"It's not exactly the movies, but there's this place I think you'll love."

Several minutes later Colin and Liv were strolling down Oxford Street, en route to Covent Garden. While they walked, they talked nonstop about everything—their families, the VJ for a Day audition, Music Mix. They easily slid back into the same natural conversation they had during their last London walk. Liv felt giddy and lighthearted as they approached the Millennium Bridge.

"Where are we going?" Liv asked as

they crossed the Thames. She could see the Tower of London off to their left, but had no idea where they were or where they were going. It was getting dark, and Liv suddenly realized they had been walking for almost two hours.

"You'll see. I just hope my uncle is there."

"Your uncle?" Liv said, stealing a glance at Colin. "Please don't tell me we're going to some sort of family picnic."

"We are not going to a family picnic. I promise." Colin smiled suspiciously and led Liv along the river. The river walk was almost deserted, and Liv was starting to feel slightly creeped out. *Does he know where he's going?* Liv wondered. Just as she was about to steal a subtle look over her shoulder to look for weird stray dogs and other creepy things, Colin turned down a short ramp and stopped. "We're here."

They were standing in front of a large round building that Liv immediately recognized from pictures as Shakespeare's Globe Theatre. "I've been dying to come here!" Liv exclaimed as Colin led her toward the entrance.

"I thought I remembered you saying how much you liked Shakespeare the first day I met you," Colin said, mirroring Liv's excitement. "I've been meaning to come here for a while—my uncle is one of the theater's prop masters, and I promised him I would pop by for a visit."

Colin led Liv inside the Globe's lobby, stopping briefly to talk to one of the staff. The clerk nodded when Colin introduced himself, and he ushered Liv and Colin through the building to the theater at the back. Liv's eyes widened as they passed replicas of Shakespeare's original Globe Theatre. Then they moved through an out-door corridor toward the stage.

They passed the main audience door and stepped into a bustling backstage area. A rosy, round man stood in the center of a circle of people, waving a sword. He looked up as Liv and Colin walked into the room, then threw his hands (which, frighteningly, still held swords) into the air and came barreling toward them. Clearly, this guy was Colin's uncle.

"M'boy!" the man exclaimed, gathering Colin into an awkward, roly-poly hug. Colin was nearly half a foot taller than his uncle, and only half as wide. Blushing, Colin introduced Liv to the man, who was—oddly—called Ginger (Colin later explained that Ginger got the nickname thanks to his red hair).

Ginger had an impossibly thick accent, and Liv—if she was being honest—couldn't understand more than ten words he was saying as he showed them around backstage. She just nodded and smiled, hoping she didn't look too stupid. Finally Ginger excused himself; a performance was under way, and he needed to outfit the cast of Romeo and Juliet with their swords and daggers. He explained, "It shan't be a bit of a tragedy without the swords, eh?"

Colin turned to Liv, laughing, as Ginger walked away. "You didn't understand anything he said, did you?"

Liv shook her head. "Not a word. Did I say anything stupid?"

"Nothing much," Colin said simply. He smiled secretly and looked like he was about to say more. But he didn't. He just motioned for her to follow as he led her into a quiet corner that was stuffed with trunks and dusty shoes. Liv suspected he was withholding something, and worried about what she might have said.

"What are you doing?" Liv whispered as Colin pried one of the trunks in the corner open. "Colin, seriously, I don't think we should take stuff."

"Not to worry, ma'am," Colin said,

winking. "You're going to have to trust me. Now . . ." He studied Liv carefully as he rustled through the trunk. "I think this will suit you nicely, yeah?"

Liv broke out laughing as Colin pulled an enormous red . . . thing . . . out of the trunk. He held it up, motioning for Liv to take the material from him. "You want me to put this, um, *frock* on?" she asked incredulously, eyeing the Renaissance-style dress.

Colin nodded and grinned, chuckling as he pawed through the trunk again. "It should fit over your clothes quite nicely. And for the gentleman . . ." Colin had pulled a long piece of checkered wool out of the trunk. "A kilt!"

"You're going to wear that?" Liv asked, giggling as Colin wrapped the material around his waist, forming a thick, unflattering skirt. She studied her dress curiously, giggling as she pulled the fabric over her head. It slipped over her T-shirt and jeans easily, and Liv poked her arms into the puffed sleeves. "How do I look?"

Colin looked up—he had been trying to secure his kilt with a large diaper pin—and burst out laughing. "I think it's missing something." Colin held up a finger as he stepped over to a rack against the wall. "A hat should complete the look." He held an enormous, wide-brimmed hat out to Liv and moved toward her to fasten the ties under her chin.

Liv studied Colin's face as he stood in front of her. His brow was furrowed, and he had pushed his lower lip out while he concentrated on unknotting the chin strap on Liv's hat. He looked up at her in the dim backstage light and smiled. His eyes were bright with laughter.

Liv broke into a smile. She felt completely silly and comfortable with Colin. Standing there in her enormous dress, watching Colin tie an Elizabethan hat around her head, Liv suddenly felt a flip in her stomach. *No!* she instructed herself. *Things are only this easy because you're* friends. *Nothing more!*

"There you go. All set," Colin said, moving away from Liv. "A hat for me," he said, quickly pulling a floppy felt hat from the rack, "and we're on our way!"

"On our way where?" Liv said, envisioning her and Colin strolling down the river walk in full costume. She hoped that wasn't what he had in mind—Colin was turning out to be even stranger than Liv.

"The theater, of course," Colin answered, poking a feather into the brim of his hat. "We missed the first act, but I believe you said you have never seen Shakespeare live?"

"I haven't. But how . . . ?"

"While you were busy nodding at everything he said, Ginger offered us seats to tonight's performance. You nodded, so I just figured . . . unless you don't want to go? It's not a comedy, but . . ." Colin tipped his hat at Liv and waited for a response.

"Of course I want to go!" Liv couldn't believe Ginger had offered them seats and she had hastily accepted. She felt really greedy, but was relieved she had been nodding, rather than shaking her head. "Shall we?"

Decked out in their silly costumes, Liv and Colin made their way through the back corridors of the Globe. Ginger had arranged a secret backstage platform for them to watch the show from. They were slightly behind and to the side of the action onstage, but Liv couldn't have been happier. She was wearing goofy clothes and watching Shakespeare from backstage at the Globe Theatre. In all her life, she could never have imagined she would *ever* be doing this.

As the curtain rose to start the second act, Liv turned to smile at Colin. "Thank you," she whispered.

He tipped his hat again. "Happy July Fourth," he whispered back. He settled into his seat and spread his kilt out around him. "You look lovely in a frock."

Love Is a Battlefield

"You!" Simon Brown bellowed in the general direction of the hallway. "Here!" Liv smiled. She had grown accustomed to Brown's no-nonsense ways, and was even starting to warm to his brusque way of summoning her to his office. It probably helped that she had been in a particularly good mood since her trip to the Globe on Friday too.

"Yes, Brown?" Liv popped her head into Brown's office and greeted him with a big smile. He looked up from his newspaper with a surly expression and cringed when he saw Liv's smile—Brown didn't like positive moods.

"Take that ridiculous expression off your

face. Are you tipsy?" Without waiting for an answer, he gave a dismissive wave. "I don't care. Anyway, you need to do something for me." He scanned a pile of papers on the corner of his desk. "We are producing a ridiculous program about the eighties. Complete rubbish, but . . ." He trailed off, muttering.

Liv waited patiently in his doorway. When a full thirty seconds had passed, she prompted him. "What can I do for you, Brown? I'm happy to help any way I can." Liv couldn't believe those words had just come out of her mouth. She sounded like a robot.

"Oh, yes, you. Right. I need you to do some research. Get me up to speed on some of the songs that made the eighties 'so bloody great.'" He made little quotes in the air. "Put something together, pull some information. Make me look good. The regular nonsense." He glanced up at Liv to make sure she was paying attention, then sighed dramatically.

"Okay," Liv said happily. "This sounds great. Do you—?"

"Go, Girl!"

Liv spun on her heel and moved away from Brown's door. Apparently there would be no further explanation. Even still, Liv could hardly contain her excitement. *Yesssss!* she thought giddily. *A real project! And it's perfect!* She had finally been asked to do something meaningful, to show Brown that she could do more than herd a roomful of freakish fans into their seats. Of course, she needed a little translation from Gloria (she had no idea what "make me look good" or "the regular nonsense" meant), but that should be no biggie.

A few minutes later Liv was standing in the Music Mix lobby, explaining the assignment.

"This is huge, Liv," Gloria said, after Liv finished reciting Brown's instructions. "He must really trust you."

Liv beamed. "Really?"

"Trust me, I would know," Gloria said, rolling her eyes. "You know I was his intern a few years ago, right?"

"For real?" Liv said, curious. "I had no idea. Was he this hard on you, too?"

"Oh, yeah. The thing is, he's actually a pretty great fellow if you can see past his creepy, self-centered exterior." Gloria laughed. "But seriously—this research he's asked you to do . . . it's a big deal. He never let me do anything more than make copies and file." Liv listened carefully as Gloria elaborated on Brown's hasty instructions—she wanted to make sure she got this right. And Gloria was an expert on Brown translation.

At the end of the following day, Liv returned to Brown's office, report in hand. She had spent two days gathering every interesting factoid about the eighties she could find. She had included little biographies of each of the major producers from the era, as well as photos and bios of each musician who had earned a number one spot on the Billboard charts.

She had also downloaded a bunch of music from iTunes (using Gloria's corporate card, which she hoped wouldn't get her friend in trouble), and burned CDs that featured each of the weekly chart toppers. Liv was excited about her report and CDs, and she stood in Simon Brown's door with a smile plastered across her face.

"Yes?" Brown didn't look up.

"I finished the report you asked me to do on the eighties," Liv said, moving toward his desk.

"Leave it," Brown said, motioning to the corner of his desk. Liv did as she was told, then retreated to her tollbooth to wait for his thoughts. The phone was ringing when she got there. Liv assumed it was her father calling to check in—he was the only person who ever called her at work. Seeing that her caller ID was an outside number, she hastily picked up the receiver and prepared herself for a long conversation.

"Hey, dad," she said, twirling her hair with her free hand.

"Well, that's an interesting nickname," the voice on the other end said, teasing. "Most girls just call me Josh, but you've always been a little different, Olivia."

Liv blushed, relieved that Josh Cameron couldn't see her at that moment. "Hi," Liv said, grinning. "I thought it was my dad. But, um, it isn't. It's you. So. How have you been?"

"It's been a while," Josh Cameron responded. Liv could hear the smile in his voice. "I've missed you."

"Me too," Liv said honestly. "Where have you been?" Liv groaned, realizing how needy and stalkerish that may have sounded.

"I've been in the States. But I'm back now. When can I see you?"

Liv's throat was dry. *Um, now?* she answered silently. "How about this weekend?"

Josh Cameron agreed, and they settled

on Saturday night. He was going to call her on Friday to work out the details—and he had given Liv his cell phone number, just in case. Hanging up, Liv couldn't stop smiling. She was going out with him again. She was going out with *Josh Cameron. Again!*

As she sat at her tollbooth, giddily reflecting on the conversation, Simon Brown sauntered over. He had *never* come to Liv's desk—his laziness prevented him from leaving his office—so she didn't really know what to do. Could she just sit there, or did she need to stand? Was she supposed to offer him her chair?

Brown solved the mystery by perching on the edge of Liv's desk, forcing her to back her chair up against the wall to give him room.

"Well done," Simon Brown said at last. "I'm impressed with your efforts." Liv could tell it had taken all of Brown's energy to dole out a compliment, which made his praise even more valuable.

"Thank you, Brown," she said, restraining herself from screaming with excitement.

"One more thing," Brown said, studying the contents of Liv's desk. "Will you be auditioning for the VJ for a Day contest?"

"Yes, sir . . . uh, Brown. Yes, Anna and I are planning to audition."

"Very well, then," Brown said, smiling slightly. His tan teeth glinted in the fluorescent light. "Very well."

As Brown sauntered off, retreating again to the confines of his office, Liv did a little dance at her tollbooth. She had done a good job. And unless she was totally misreading him, Liv was pretty sure Simon Brown had—in his strange, confusing way—just endorsed her VJ for a Day audition. At the very least, he wasn't totally against her auditioning.

And that alone was something.

That Friday, Liv was still floating. Brown had retreated back into his crabby shell, but now Liv knew that he wasn't totally out to get her. He hadn't stopped acting crass and rude, but at least he had shown Liv—if only for a minute—that he was the tiniest bit human inside.

She was distracted all morning, obsessing about her date with Josh Cameron the next day. She couldn't prevent her nerves from going crazy every time she thought about hanging out with him. She assumed things would get more natural between them soon—at least, that's what she was hoping. *I won't be intimidated by his celebrity status forever, right?* she wondered over a midmorning latte. *He's the same as everyone else—just a little more . . . famous. But I know that doesn't really mean anything.*

Liv had started to realize her obsession with celebrity was silly—now that she had spent a few weeks surrounded by stars and their entourages at Music Mix, she had seen firsthand how *average* most of them were. Usually they just had a touch more attitude.

Celebrities are just people who got lucky and had their talent turned into fame. So why did they deserve her respect and admiration so much more than, say, someone like Anna did? When she thought about it that way, Liv realized that she would much rather spend an evening with Anna than with someone famous *just* because they're famous. At least with her friends, she was comfortable being herself. She didn't worry about whether she was doing and saying the right things.

Liv realized she had been nervous around Josh Cameron for all the wrong reasons. When she let herself just *be*, things were always so much smoother and less awkward. She needed to let down her guard and hang out with him as an equal—not as Josh Cameron, *Superstar,* and Olivia Phillips, *Who?*

But before she could test out her new theory, Liv was forced to deal with one more celebrity ego—and this one made it tougher for her to remain calm and natural. Friday afternoon, Liv was summoned to the studio where Cherie Jacobson, Josh Cameron's ex, was in rehearsal. Cherie was scheduled to perform on *Hits Parade* in just a few hours, and Liv was dying to see what she was like.

Part of Liv didn't want to meet her new boyfriend's ex, but the other part of her was desperately curious. Liv figured there was no way Cherie knew about her and Josh Cameron's relationship—it's not like they'd been out in public together after that first date—but her stomach was in knots nonetheless.

Cherie's new single was a response to Josh Cameron's single, "Split," and rumored to be harsh. Their breakup had been smeared through the tabloids, and Cherie had gotten most of the bad press. Apparently, she had gone psycho, and frankly, Liv was a little scared of her.

When Liv got to the studio, she quietly poked her head in to catch the attention of one of Cherie's assistants. A tall, rail-thin woman came to the door and ushered Liv inside. Cherie stood in the center of the *Hits Parade* stage, red hair flowing down her back as she belted out the last notes of her song. When the music ended, she returned the microphone gently to its stand and smiled at Liv.

"Hi, sweetie," she said, her voice dripping kindness. "Thanks for coming by. I hear you're the girl to go to when I need something?"

That's me, Liv thought, already annoyed. *Waitress, dog groomer, maid—at your service. There's that celebrity attitude.* Out loud, she said, "Yep. What can I do for you?"

"What you can do," Cherie said, all kindness stripped from her voice, "is lay your hands off my boyfriend." Liv's knees buckled. "I have friends everywhere, and they tell me everything. Just to remind you, you're nobody. And I can make your life miserable."

Liv stared at Cherie Jacobson. "Excuse me?" Liv said, much more boldly than she had intended. For some reason, she suddenly wasn't intimidated.

Cherie's smile returned to her face, and the false charm that had been there earlier snuck back into her voice. "What I mean to say is," she said, putting her hand on Liv's arm, "be careful. You don't know what you're dealing with." And with that, she spun on her heel and returned to the Green Room.

Liv headed out of the studio. As she walked down the hall, she considered Cherie's warning. She was a little flattered that Cherie was threatened by her, but equally freaked out. She didn't want anything to put a damper on the next day's date with Josh Cameron. . . . but what had Cherie meant when she said, "You don't know what you're dealing with"?

You're So Vain

Liv stood in line at the half-price theater ticket booth at Leicester Square, soaked and miserable. She hadn't realized that the ticket office didn't open until eleven, and she'd been waiting to buy tickets for almost two hours.

Stupidly, she hadn't brought an umbrella. And shortly after she had settled into her place near the front of the line, the sky had opened up and poured for twenty minutes straight. She had nonchalantly tried to duck under her neighbor's umbrella, but when the man in front of her saw her inching closer and closer, he had freaked out and vacated the line. The bad news was that she had lost her only hope of staying dry. The good news was that she had moved up in line.

The rain had eventually slowed to a drizzle, but the damage was done. Liv was cranky, dripping wet, and completely void of any remaining patience. Finally, a few minutes after eleven, the booth opened and she approached the window.

"Two tickets to *As You Like It*, please." Liv smiled at the booth attendant and waited.

"I have two tickets in the first row of the second balcony. Okay?"

Liv wasn't sure. The truth was, she didn't know why she had agreed to do this in the first place. Why, when Josh Cameron had called and asked her out again, had she insisted on planning the date? He was a multimillionaire, and she was . . . well, *not* a multimillionaire. In fact, these tickets were going to cost her an entire week's salary. She could only hope that he would pay for the rest of the date.

But, she thought, *this way I can show him what I like to do.* She was confident Josh Cameron would love Shakespeare just as much as she did, and she couldn't wait to see one of her favorite plays live onstage.

"That's fine. The first row of the balcony

is fine." Liv paid, and wandered away from the half-price booth, tickets in hand. She was worried that he would be disappointed with their seats. He probably only ever sat in the first row. Or some sort of luxury box. *Whatever,* she thought, shrugging off her paranoia. *I'm sure he's not that shallow. And he said he liked me because I'm "normal."*

Nine hours later, dry and umbrella-ed, Liv stood outside the theatre, waiting for Josh Cameron's limo to arrive. She had gotten there a few minutes before their planned meeting time, and had been waiting for twenty minutes. The play was supposed to start in less than five minutes, and Liv was starting to get nervous . . . and wet again.

Only moments before the theater doors closed, a limo came zipping around the corner. Josh Cameron hopped out of the backseat and embraced Liv in a quick hug. Several passing tourists stopped to stare and point, and a small herd of paparazzi materialized out of nowhere. Liv was taken aback, but Josh Cameron deftly stepped away and smiled for the cameras. He waved, then took Liv's arm and moved quickly into the theater.

"As usual, you look incredible," Josh

Cameron said as Liv silently led him up the stairs toward their seats. She was still stunned by the scene outside—she had never been near paparazzi before, and she was freaked that she might be *in* the pictures. "I apologize for my lateness," Josh Cameron continued.

Liv waited for a further explanation, but none was forthcoming. "It's okay," she said simply. "But we should hurry. The show's about to start."

As they settled into their seats in the second balcony, Josh Cameron looked around. People were staring, and he shifted nervously in his seat. Smiling uncomfortably, he whispered to Liv, "We're an awfully long way from the stage, aren't we?"

Liv's stomach dropped. She couldn't believe she had been so stupid as to try to arrange this. He was probably horrified that he was stuck in the back of the theater with normal people. They could barely see over the balcony edge, and they were sitting a million miles above the stage. "I'm sorry. It's all they had," she explained quietly, studying her program to avoid his eyes.

"Not to worry, Olivia," he murmured in her ear. "I just appreciate you making the effort. Like I told you before, it's nice to be normal every once and a while. And it's refreshing to go on a date that my assistant didn't plan." Then he slouched down in his seat to hide from curious onlookers. As the curtain rose, Josh Cameron slid his hand into Liv's and left it there through the rest of the play.

Liv could barely focus on *As You Like It*. Fortunately, she had read the play at least five times and easily followed the plot. But she was antsy and distracted, worrying about whether Josh Cameron was having a good time. He kept shifting anxiously in his seat, and hadn't laughed at any of the obviously funny parts.

When the final curtain dropped, Liv clapped and cheered with the rest of the crowd. Josh Cameron took his cell phone out of his pocket and quickly tapped out a text message. Liv glanced at him, and he stuffed his phone back into his pocket. When the cast took their places on the stage for the curtain call, Josh Cameron stood and led Liv out of the theater. He hurried them down the stairs and into the lobby, just as the crowds started to fill the main level of the theater.

"Let's get out of here," he said, weaving through the crowd as Liv struggled to catch up. She didn't know why they were in such a rush, but just assumed this meant that he had *not* liked the play. He held Liv's hand tightly as they moved through the crowded lobby and toward the front doors. Just as they were about to exit the theater, Liv's stomach lurched when she spotted a familiar face near one of the side doors.

"Colin!" she shouted, eager to be heard above the noisy crowd. Liv waved as Colin looked up and spotted her. Squeezing Josh Cameron's hand to get his attention, she leaned toward him and said, "Hang on one second—a friend of mine is here. I just want to say hi."

Liv crossed the lobby toward Colin with her date in tow. Her heart skipped a beat when she saw that Colin also wasn't alone— rather, he was with a gorgeous girl. *Who is she, and where is Rebecca?* Liv wondered.

Liv forced herself to shove aside the instant jealousy by focusing on Josh Cameron's hand in hers. *You are on a DATE,* she reminded herself. *With Josh Cameron. So stop being stupid. Now.*

"Liv," Colin stated simply. Liv thought he looked a little pale and uncomfortable, but couldn't be sure. "Did you enjoy the show?"

"Yeah!" Liv shouted, a little too loudly and awkwardly for her taste. "Oh, umm, have you guys met? Josh Cameron, this is Colin Johnstone."

"Colin, is it?" Josh Cameron said. Liv thought she caught him sizing up Colin's date, but chose to pretend she hadn't. "You don't actually like this stuff, do you, mate?" He motioned in the direction of the stage and laughed. Liv's hunch had been correct. Josh Cameron did not like Shakespeare. *Marvelous.*

"Yes, it's Colin," Colin responded coldly, glancing at Liv. "And yes, I love 'this stuff.'" Liv shifted uncomfortably. Colin continued, "Liv, this is Lucy. Lucy, Liv." Liv shook hands with Lucy, curious about who the mystery date was.

A few seconds of awkward silence passed, then Josh Cameron broke in. "Well, this has been fun. Olivia, are you ready?" Liv nodded, and he turned to address Colin and Lucy. "We're off to the 400 Bar—I'm thinking of doing a little impromptu performance tonight. We'll see, people may get lucky." He winked and flashed his dimples. "If you would like to join us, I guess I can *try* to . . ."

Colin broke in, "We have other plans.

Thanks for the generous offer." Liv groaned quietly. This meeting was not going well. *Why,* she wondered, *were both guys acting so rude?*

"It was nice to meet you, Liv," Lucy said kindly. She nodded at Josh Cameron, then linked her hand around Colin's arm and led him out of the theater.

As Liv followed Josh Cameron out of the theater's front doors, she briefly debated asking him why he had been so rude to her friend. She also considered asking him if it would have been so difficult to *try* to enjoy the date she had planned. But she didn't ask. She just followed him silently through the after-theater crowd and into his waiting limo. She sat quietly in one corner of the car while Josh Cameron made several calls, figuring out which club was hot that night.

"The 400 Bar it is," he exclaimed eventually, flipping his phone closed. "The club owner is totally into me trying out my new single tonight." His face was flushed, and he suddenly looked much more like a little kid than an international pop star.

"That's great," she said hollowly, sinking into her seat across from him. "What's the new single called?"

"It's a remix of 'You're So Vain,' the

Carly Simon song. You know the one?" He hummed a few bars of the song. Liv certainly did know the one, and smiled at the irony of the song's title. It somehow seemed just perfect for Josh Cameron. "I'm trying to work it out before my Music Mix concert. It's nice to try it out for my peeps, you know?" He paused, tapping out another text message. "All right! We're here!" Josh Cameron pushed open his door and hopped out of the limo. He turned, checking to see that Liv was following him.

Inside the 400 Bar, the lights were low and the floors were grimy. It was the opposite of Meat by appearance standards, but the people were equally intimidating. Liv had still not gotten used to the VIP scene. She could feel everyone staring at her, and she felt like a complete clod. She had worn a thin sweater and chinos to the theater, and realized now how ridiculous she must look wearing Gap at a trendy bar.

Liv followed Josh through the crowd to a small bar across the room. Josh Cameron rested his arm on the jukebox against the wall and waved to a half-dressed bartender pouring a beer. She sauntered over, planting a kiss firmly on Josh Cameron's mouth. He chuckled; Liv gawked.

"What's up, El?" he asked the bartender, flashing a quick smile at Liv, who was still dwelling on the strange and unexpected kiss.

"Hey, Joshie," she responded with a thick Irish accent. "We've been waiting for you. Tracy!" She called to a large, bald man on the other end of the bar. The man—Liv could only assume this was Tracy—moved toward them. Wordlessly, he slid the jukebox away from its place on the wall, revealing a door that had been hidden behind it. Liv stared as Tracy pulled a large ring of keys off his belt and slid one into the old-fashioned lock on the wooden door. With a whine, the door slid open.

Looking through the hidden door, Liv could only see feet and legs. The bottom half of the door opening was sealed up with concrete, and the top half opened onto the floor level of another room. It appeared that the room behind the door was about three feet higher than the room they were currently in, and they would need to shimmy through a tiny little opening if they were going to enter it. As Liv stared in confusion, Josh hoisted himself up and slid into the secret room.

Suddenly Liv's feet left the ground.

Tracy had lifted and spun her toward the door's opening. Before she had a chance to react, she was sitting on the floor of the other room, and the secret door was closed behind her. Liv could hear the jukebox sliding back into its place against the wall. She was trapped.

Standing up, Liv scanned the hidden bar they had just entered. Gone were the grimy, soiled floors and dark, depressing lighting. This bar was snazzy and clean, complete with smooth tiled floors and shimmery lighting. A low bench ran around the perimeter of the room, but it was empty. Most of the people in the room were dancing or mingling around the bar, clustered in small groups. Each group had at least one person whom Liv recognized as some sort of celebrity—including Bethany Jameson and Christy Trimble, the starlets she had first met at Meat. Luckily, Cherie Jacobson was nowhere in sight.

Josh Cameron had disappeared, leaving Liv to fend for herself. It suddenly felt like she had turned up at her high school prom with her dress tucked into her underwear and no date.

Luckily, most people in the bar hadn't really noticed her, so she took a moment to wander around the room and check it out.

She noticed that one wall was a panel of murky glass that looked over the bar they had originally entered. Liv assumed that they were, once again, in some sort of VIP section, and the lower-level bar on the other side of the jukebox was the "regular" area of the club.

"Hello, you." Josh Cameron had sauntered up behind Liv while she was looking through the window at the crowds of people on the other side of the hidden door. "Pretty incredible, isn't it?" Liv turned around, and he planted a soft kiss on her lips. Nuzzling into her neck, he continued, "This club is great for trying out new songs because we can see how the crowd responds on the dance floor." He gestured to the windows.

Liv decided not to tell him how creepy she thought that sounded. *This is like Pop Star Big Brother or something.* Her discomfort seemed to melt away as she relaxed into his arms. Liv wasn't really into the VIP club scene, but she liked having Josh Cameron's attention shining upon her. Maybe she could get used to the scene—if it meant more people noticing Josh Cameron noticing *her*. He kissed her again and a stray curl brushed against Liv's cheek.

"Well, baby," he said, breaking the

moment with a quick kiss on the cheek. "You have fun. I've got some people I need to talk to. . . ." With that, he worked his way back into the crowd and left Liv alone again.

For the next three hours Liv sat patiently in the corner of the room while Josh Cameron worked the club, meeting, greeting, and schmoozing. She had—awkwardly—tried to join him a few times, but he had mostly ignored her. So each time, after a few minutes of standing or dancing on the outside of a circle of celebrities, she retreated back to her spot on one of the benches overlooking the lower bar.

She had never felt more like a boring, out-of-place loser than she did that night. She self-consciously adjusted her sweater periodically, attempting to lower the neckline to give herself a slightly more stylish look, but it was useless. No matter what she did to physically fit in, she would just never click in this world.

Just as Liv began to drift off to sleep (her cushioned bench had been too tempting, and she was Bored Bored Bored), Liv spotted her "date" coming her way. She smiled weakly as he slid up next to her. *Finally.*

"You," Josh Cameron said, poking Liv's

nose softly, "are such a sweetheart for understanding that I have people to talk to and things to take care of." He ran a hand through his hair. "You know, it's so much easier dating a regular girl than a celebrity. I mean, it's amazing that you don't really have your own stuff to take care of—that way, it's cool for you to just sit here and chill."

Liv stared at him. *Did I just hear that right? I "don't have my own stuff" to do? I can just "sit here and chill"?! Am I a lapdog or something?*

"And," Josh Cameron continued, his dimples deepening, "dating you will do wonders for my image after Cherie. I've really come out of this breakup looking like the normal one, haven't I?" He leaned over to kiss Liv, but she quickly stood up before he could get within six inches. She had—officially—had it.

"Josh," she began, "yes, I am just a 'regular girl,' and yes, I have been patient while you've ignored me all night. But normal people do have lives. And I do, contrary to your opinion, have plenty of things I would be *much* happier doing. So while you may think that dating me will be good for your image, I don't think that dating you will be good for me." She paused to take a breath. "I thank you for *gracing* me with your presence over the past few weeks, but now I have *very* important things I need to attend to. And *this* is just not worth my time. So good night."

And with that, she pushed through the crowd, knocked on the secret door, and slid through the hole and out of her VIP existence.

Sunglasses at Night

Josh Cameron had called Liv at work several times in the days following her Girl Power moment, but Liv resisted his charms. On their final date, she had realized she didn't like the person she was when she was with him, and she hated that she felt so powerless around him. Liv had avoided her gut instinct the first few times they had gone out, but now she realized the celeb lifestyle wasn't for her, anyway—she wanted to feel comfortable being herself. And while Josh Cameron claimed to love her honesty and "all-American, real girl" ways, she just couldn't get into being the novelty date.

The only bad thing about the breakup was that Liv had plenty of time to dwell on her now obvious—and depressingly unreciprocated—crush on Colin. She thought constantly about their run-in at the theater, disgusted by how rude Josh Cameron had been to him.

Liv was dying to know who Colin's mystery date had been that night. She had been tempted to ask Rebecca, but figured that was probably not the nicest thing to do. Either Rebecca knew about Lucy and chose to ignore her, or Liv would be the bearer of really awkward news. In spite of her relationship with Rebecca, Liv felt sorry for her roommate—did she know about Lucy?

One night that week, after a particularly grueling day at work, Liv decided to stop off at Tully's for a cup of tea. She had spent her day running around town looking for a particular brand of snack bar. One of Music Mix's performers had brought his girlfriend to the set with him, and she was craving some special Australian snack bar that she missed from home . . . so Liv was sent out to fetch one for her. After checking every sandwich shop and market around Oxford Street, Liv had finally found the bar more than five hours later at an Australian sweater shop in Notting Hill. By the time she got back to the studio, the guest and his girl were gone. *A day well spent,* she mused.

She breezed into Tully's and was greeted warmly by the woman behind the counter. As she waited for her tea, the frustrations of her day quickly fading, Liv was startled by someone tapping on her shoulder. Turning, she was pleased to see Colin. She had run into him at Tully's a million times that summer—when she was on cappuccino runs for Green Room guests and he was satisfying Andrew Stone's soy latte addiction—but seeing him startled her, considering how much she'd been thinking about him that week. "Oh, hi," she said, noticing a flush creeping up her cheeks.

"Hi, Liv. All right?"

"Yeah, good. You?" *This is awkward,* Liv thought, cringing. *Why?* Before he could say anything more, she continued. "You know, I've been looking for you all week. I just wanted to apologize for my, um, date last weekend—he was a real jerk to you at *As You Like It.* I'm sorry."

"Liv, you don't need to apologize for him. Unless you were telling him what to say, it really wasn't your fault."

"Thanks. But it's my fault he was there,

so I guess I feel somehow responsible." She paused. "So, ah, did you enjoy the play?"

"Yeah, it was great." Colin turned to collect his order from the counter. Liv noticed two cups, and glanced quickly around the room. She spotted Lucy, the girl from the play, gazing out the window at a table across the room. Colin's jacket was draped over the back of the chair next to hers. He continued, "We loved it."

Liv grimaced. There it was—"we." Liv knew it wasn't any of her business, but she was just dying to know how this girl fit into Colin's relationship with Rebecca. Liv suddenly felt oddly protective of her roommate, and didn't want to see her get hurt. She couldn't stop herself from blurting out, "So . . . how are things with you and Rebecca?"

Colin groaned. "Man, I knew you were going to ask me that." Liv nodded, watching Lucy out of the corner of her eye. "Rebecca and I are *not* together, if that's what you're implying."

Liv raised her eyebrows. "Really?"

"Definitely. Rebecca is very much *not* my type. But I do value her as a friend. I know that might sound crazy, but she's really very sweet, and there's something about her that just makes me laugh."

"Yeah, something about her makes me laugh too," Liv said sarcastically, setting her tea down on the nearest table. Colin hovered next to her table as Liv poured milk in her tea and stirred.

Colin continued, "The thing you should probably know is, in our first week in London, Rebecca really confided in me. She was worried she wasn't fitting in, and felt like she couldn't get along with you or Anna. She felt like an outsider, and I think she thought that spending time with me might give her credibility or something." He paused. "I liked hanging out with her. It's not a pity thing—she's really funny, if you get past that petty, selfish exterior. I just don't know if she's that great with other girls, yeah?"

"Yeah," Liv agreed. "I think that might be a fair assessment." She didn't know why she was being so rude, but she couldn't stop herself. *It's not Rebecca's fault I missed my chance with Colin,* Liv mused. *I'm the only one to blame for that.*

Colin was still holding both cups of tea and had begun to fidget. He said quietly, "But I think she also sort of thought that if she and I spent time together, it might make you jealous." Colin paused. "But that's ridiculous, considering . . ."

"Considering what?" Liv asked, curious.

"Considering . . . other relationships." Colin looked down at his feet, then glanced at Lucy. "Right . . . ," he said, suddenly awkward. "Well, our tea is getting cold."

"Yeah, you should probably get back." Liv couldn't believe she'd been so wrong about Colin and Rebecca. "It was good to see you, Colin. Again, I'm sorry about the whole Josh Cameron thing last weekend."

"No problem," Colin said. "I'm sure he's a really great guy once you get to know him." And then he lifted one of the teacups in a little wave and strolled back to his table.

"Ah was talking to some of the producers from the events team, and they are just pos-ah-ti-uhv that I will win this little VJ for a Day contest." Rebecca delicately sipped her coffee, and studied Liv's reaction.

"That's great, Rebecca," Liv said blandly, for what felt like the thousandth time that night. "I'm really happy for you."

Earlier that evening Liv and Anna had decided they needed a girls' night out. Feeling generous, they had invited Rebecca to join them. Liv had thought a lot about what Colin had told her about Rebecca, and felt guilty that Rebecca hadn't made many friends in London. She really didn't want to be part of the reason someone was so unhappy, and she had vowed to try to give her roommate another chance.

About ten minutes after they left the office, Liv had regretted her generosity. Rebecca hadn't stopped talking, and most of their conversations for the past two hours had centered on Rebecca's brilliance. And, much to Liv's dismay, Rebecca refused to stop talking about the VJ for a Day contest. The good thing about Liv's breakup with Josh Cameron was that it had freed up plenty of time for her and Anna to focus on their audition material. They had finally formulated the beginning of a plan, and had been working almost nonstop to perfect it. Liv was confident that they would have a great segment ready in time for the auditions in a few weeks, but that didn't mean she was any more excited about listening to Rebecca's take on the auditions.

As Rebecca chattered on, bragging about her "fab-u-lous" ideas for her audition, Liv and Anna finished their drinks and stood up to leave. Rebecca didn't miss a beat. She continued to talk while sweeping My Rover into her arms (she had somehow gotten away with bringing Hell Dog to work for "show and teh-ull" that day).

Then she drained her coffee and dropped her Gucci sunglasses back into place on her perky little nose. Liv couldn't figure out why Rebecca was wearing sunglasses at night, but, considering Liv's own fashion expertise, figured she really wasn't the best person to criticize someone else's style.

The three flatmates made their way outside and headed for the tube at Piccadilly Circus. "Ah don't know if you know this, but I actually won the Junior Miss contest in Texas." Rebecca fixed Anna and Liv with a serious stare through her Guccis.

"I never would have guessed," Liv muttered to herself. Anna heard her and started giggling.

"They told me I was a natural onstage." Rebecca held My Rover up to her face and pushed her lips out to give him a kiss. She continued in a baby voice, addressing My Rover. "So I just *know* I'm going to be the very best VJ that Music Mix has ever seen. Look out England—Miss Texas is here!" Rebecca smiled widely, revealing her perfect white teeth. Liv wondered if Rebecca put Vaseline on her teeth in real life, like they do in pageants. They were unnaturally shiny.

"You know, Li-uhv," Rebecca said sweetly, pausing as they passed the Piccadilly Circus fountain. "Maybe you could just help me with *my* audition. Work behind the scenes or something? Ah mean, I just don't want it to be uncomfortable for y'all when I win." Rebecca pulled a coin out of her clutch. "Lucky penny. Here's to my win!" she said, lowering her ridiculous sunglasses to wink as she tossed the coin over her shoulder into the fountain. Then she walked up the steps to the fountain base platform and started strutting around the edge.

As she listened to Rebecca ramble on, Liv considered the question she had been asking herself all night. *Was Colin right about Rebecca? Why would she come out with us unless she actually likes us better than she lets on?*

Liv was jolted out of her head by a high-pitched squeal. She turned back toward the fountain just in time to see Rebecca teetering madly, her high heel stuck in a crack in the concrete. Flailing her arms, Rebecca buckled sideways and landed right in the Piccadilly Circus fountain. Several groups of tourists, out for a late-night stroll, quickly grabbed their cameras and snapped pictures. "Ah'm okay!" Rebecca said, flashing her pearly whites just before her hair hit the water. "Ah've got My Rover and my Guccis—I'm okay!"

Liv watched, horrified, as Rebecca floundered in the fountain. She was trying to keep her sunglasses and My Rover in the air. As Liv moved to help her out of the fountain, she could see tears of humiliation welling up in Rebecca's eyes.

For once, Liv felt genuine empathy for her flatmate. *She* is *normal,* Liv thought. *She's desperate for attention and doesn't know how to treat people, but she's not immune to humiliation.* In that moment Liv suddenly realized that under Rebecca's thick veneer of I Love Myself-itis, she was just as self-conscious and awkward as anyone else. Rebecca just hadn't figured out a normal way of dealing with it.

She may be annoying and weird and talk about herself way too much, Liv thought, *but maybe she just needs people to be nice to her so she can realize she's safe being herself.* Looking at her soaked and tear-drenched flatmate floundering in the fountain, Liv vowed to give Rebecca another chance—for real, this time. Reaching out her hand to take My Rover from Rebecca's slippery, wet arm, Liv smiled. "Are you okay?" she asked, true concern ringing in her voice.

Rebecca looked up at Liv as a tear rolled down her face. "Ah'm fine. Thank you," she smiled. "Li-uhv, can you please dry My Rover's ears? He's prone to infection."

You Spin Me Round (Like a Record)

"Have you ever heard the theory that people and their pets look alike?" Liv was sitting in a small windowless room, surrounded by no fewer than twenty assorted dogs, cats, and one very loud parakeet.

Anna, who was squatting by her side, straightened the hood on a greyhound's zip-up sweater and nodded. "I have heard that."

"Don't you think Josh Cameron's dog looks just like him?" Liv giggled, gesturing to a black cocker spaniel that was lying on a cushy armchair in the corner of the room, surveying the rest of the dogs with pity. "The curls, the charming look, the snobby attitude—it's all there. Poor dog. I have to say, every time I look at that dog, I freak out just a little. It's frightening how similar they look."

Liv had totally gotten over Josh Cameron, but couldn't stop a hint of bitterness from creeping up—in part, because she had been assigned the worst possible task at that night's Josh Cameron concert. Over the past two weeks the only thing anyone at Music Mix had talked about was the approaching concert, and now that concert was finally here.

Lucky Liv had found herself assigned to the charming job of tending to Josh Cameron's dog and his backup dancers' pets during rehearsal and the concert. Which is why she was, at that moment, locked in the pet-bed room she herself had prepared a few weeks before—along with twenty unruly, high-attitude designer pets.

Anna had volunteered to accompany Liv to the concert to help out—she hadn't gotten an invite to the concert as part of the wardrobe team, and really wanted to see the show. Liv had asked Brown if she could bring backup, and he had—in a fit of kindness—agreed.

The two of them had been stuck in the pet room for the past two hours while Josh Cameron and his dancers rehearsed and relaxed in style. Liv and Anna's Animal

House was not quite as plush—each of the dogs and cats had a squishy bed or pillow, but Liv and Anna were forced to sit on the floor. There were no human-size accommodations in sight.

As Liv prepared doggie dinners, Simon Brown poked his head into the circus and gestured to Liv. "You," he barked. "You're needed at the stage. It seems one of the dancers couldn't part with her pooch until the show started. I refuse to have that . . . *creature* . . . crawling out onstage during the show. So you will collect it from her and hustle back here. Go, Girl!"

Liv groaned. This chore would potentially involve her running into Josh Cameron, which she had been trying to avoid. So far she had succeeded—her Pet Land headquarters had certainly been a good hiding place. But she supposed she couldn't avoid it all night, and she hustled off down the hall in search of the rogue pet.

In the darkened hallway Liv literally ran into Christy Trimble. Christy was widely known to be the fiercest celebrity on the pop circuit, and everyone tried to stay on her good side. Liv suspected her rather loud outburst at the 400 Bar hadn't left her in Christy's good graces.

"Olivia, isn't it?" Christy asked, surveying Liv's pet hair–covered jeans and T-shirt. "I've been hoping I would see you again."

Uh-oh.

Christy continued, "Your little 'exchange' with Josh Cameron at the 400 Bar a few weeks ago . . ." She made little quotes in the air with her perfectly manicured fingers, then broke into a smile. "Well done. I haven't seen anyone stand up to Josh like that before. I'm impressed."

"Oh," Liv said, flustered. "Uh, thanks. Really?"

"Really. That speech of yours was priceless. He needed that. And, despite what the gossip rags say, Cherie Jacobson is a good friend of mine. I filled her in on your little outburst, and she got a huge kick out of it. She thinks you're fabulous now, and wanted me to pass along her congratulations. You were a hit, girl.

"If you ever need anything, give me a call." Christy hastily scribbled out her cell phone number on a piece of paper and stuffed it into Liv's jeans pocket. "I mean it. Anything, anytime. I like you—you have spunk." With a wink, Christy turned and strutted down the hall.

Liv laughed in disbelief, and wandered

over to the stage area. As she walked through the wings, Liv heard Rebecca before she saw her. Rebecca had been given the opportunity to introduce Josh Cameron to the audience—a reward from the producers on the events team, apparently—and she hadn't stopped gloating about it all week. Now Rebecca was standing just off to one side of the stage, swooshing her hair and rehearsing.

"Y'all, please welcome Josh Cameron!" Liv cringed when she heard Rebecca's drawl. As Liv poked her head around a curtain to see if the backup dancers were anywhere nearby, Rebecca spotted her and motioned her to come over.

"Oh, Li-uhv," she gushed. "Ah just can't wait to do this. I'm ready!" Liv was a little frightened—Rebecca seemed a lot like a cheerleader. A psycho cheerleader. There was something unsettling about how much enthusiasm she seemed to have about doing this introduction.

"Are you nervous?" Liv asked, only mildly curious. If she had to get up onstage in front of thousands of people, she would be freaked out. Her performance on the catwalk at Runway had been hard enough. But Liv suspected Rebecca wouldn't show weakness, even if she were mortified.

"Not one teeny tiny little bit," Rebecca said. Liv thought she saw a hint of terror cross Rebecca's face, but it was immediately covered by another huge grin and a hair toss.

Just as Liv was about to excuse herself to continue her quest for the missing dog, the lights dimmed and the crowd started cheering. The concert was about to start.

"Oh gosh, Li-uhv," Rebecca said, grabbing Liv's arm tightly for support. "Please don't leave me. It's almost time." Liv studied Rebecca's face in the dim light. The self-composed Rebecca that had been next to her a second before was gone—she had been replaced by a panic-stricken, teary-eyed mess.

Liv could hear the band tuning behind the curtain onstage. She and Rebecca were shooed to the side as the backup dancers filed past and into their places onstage. One dancer hastily dumped a pug (who was wearing a PUG REVOLUTION T-shirt) into Liv's arms as she passed. Just as Josh Cameron sauntered past them and up the stairs to the stage (without so much as a glance in Liv's direction), a producer approached Rebecca with a microphone and announced, "You're on. Go!"

Pug in hand, Liv turned to wish Rebecca good luck. That's when she realized something was desperately wrong. Rebecca had turned a nauseating shade of green. "Oh, Li-uhv," she whined. "Ah just can't do this. You go." Then she handed Liv the microphone and pleaded with her eyes.

"No way," Liv said, pushing the mic toward Rebecca. "This is what you've been waiting for!"

"Ah can't! Ah swear." Rebecca was quaking with fear. "Please go, Li-uhv."

Realizing there were very few options—*someone* had to introduce the jerk—Liv took the microphone and moved up the stairs to the stage. She had no idea what she was supposed to do, but figured she could wing it. She gently pulled aside a small section of the curtain. The pug—which was still under one arm—whined as the roar of the crowd crept around the edge of the curtain. *Gulp.*

Liv gingerly moved onto the stage. She was greeted by thousands of screaming, applauding fans. Before she could freak herself out any further, Liv leaned into the microphone and shouted, "Hello, London!" Huge applause. "Music Mix is proud to present . . ." She lifted the pug into the air. ". . . Josh Cameron!"

The crowd roared. Liv had survived. Taking a deep breath, she moved behind the curtain. As she passed Josh Cameron on her way offstage, he smiled at her and gave her a little wink. Liv winked back—and realized he didn't intimidate her anymore. She finally felt like they were on the same level. Before jogging offstage, she turned and said calmly, "Good luck out there . . . Josh."

"So it turns out, our favorite roommate is mortified of public speaking," Liv said. She and Anna were sitting in a banquette at the concert's wrap party later that night. Gloria had convinced Brown to rent out a nearby club to congratulate the Music Mix crew on a job well done and to impress Josh Cameron and his dancers—Brown had agreed it was a good idea after the pop star had agreed to attend the party. Now most of the interns were packed onto the dance floor trying to get near him—Liv did not feel inspired to join them.

"I think tonight probably ruined her chances for the VJ for a Day audition," Anna said, stretching back into the booth. "If she really was planning to audition—I wonder if it was all just for show?"

"You're right," Liv said thoughtfully.

"This may sound crazy, but do you think there's any way we could work *with* her? We *could* use her help with the makeup and hair. Right?"

"Aha," Anna said knowingly. "A plan."

"A plan." Now that Liv thought about it, asking Rebecca to join their VJ for a Day team was perfect—she had a lot of good ideas; she just needed to be reined in. Liv hoped their flatmate would agree to collaboration. After her humiliation at the concert earlier that evening, Liv suspected Rebecca would do anything to avoid public speaking again—and Liv knew she wouldn't easily give up a chance to win something. Liv and Anna could be her only chance.

"Liv?" Anna was looking across the dance floor at the club's front door. She pointed to two familiar figures who had just entered the party. "Is that Colin and Francesco?"

Liv glanced up. Her heart skipped a beat when she saw Colin's grin from afar. "Uh-huh."

"So," Anna said quietly. "What do you want to do?"

"I just can't believe how much I've screwed this up," Liv responded. As she did, she stood and waved Colin and Francesco over to their table. "I think I need to just try to talk to him again—at the very least, I can salvage the friendship, right? There's no need to avoid him. . . ."

Liv's stomach was in knots. She hadn't seen much of Colin since their last run-in at Tully's. He'd been really busy with work—and helping Rebecca with her VJ for a Day audition—and Liv had been spending most of her time with Anna working on their audition. Though she knew there was no hope for anything more than friendship with Colin, Liv wanted to try to preserve that. She couldn't stop thinking about how much fun they had had that summer—if she could just get her heart to stop thumping so hard every time he was nearby, she knew they could have a really great friendship.

As Colin and Francesco approached their table, Anna stood and grabbed Francesco's arm. "Francesco! *Buon giorno!* Come—dance with me!"

Not so subtle, Liv thought, cringing. But she shot her friend a grateful look, and—after a quick cheek-kiss from Francesco—turned to Colin. "Hey."

"Hello," Colin murmured, sliding into the booth beside her.

"How have you been?"

"So formal, Liv," Colin said, grinning. "It's not like you, yeah? But to answer your question, I've been good."

Liv relaxed. Clearly, this was the same old Colin. "Good. Sorry. So did you enjoy the Josh Cameron concert? Somehow I ended up onstage, introducing him. Which was awkward," Liv broke off. Of course, she just *had* to bring up Josh Cameron. *Swell, Liv, swell.*

"Awkward because . . . he's your boyfriend, yeah?"

"Oh no, no. That's done. Over. It wasn't pretty." She shrugged.

"Over?" Colin said, tilting his head.

"Yeah, I broke things off after that night at *As You Like It.*"

Did he not know that? Liv wondered, thinking back to their recent conversation at Tully's. "The thing is," she continued, her heart thumping as she realized she couldn't stop herself. "I guess I was looking for more than just a famous date—I think I'm better suited to someone who I can be myself with. But sometimes you figure that out a little too late . . . ," she broke off, and stared down at the table.

Colin sat there quietly, waiting for Liv

to continue. She flushed as he stared at her in the club lights. "But you know what?" she said boldly, looking directly at him, "I think I missed my chance with the right guy."

"I'm not so sure about that," he said, frowning. "Liv, can I ask you something?" She nodded. "Do you remember the night we went to the Globe?"

"Of course," she answered. "It's the highlight of my summer so far."

Colin looked relieved. "Well, do you remember how you kept nodding at everything my uncle asked you?" Liv nodded, hearing Ginger's thick accent in her head. She impulsively grinned at the memory of Colin in his kilt.

"Well . . . ," he said, smiling slightly. "While we were there, Ginger asked you a lot of strange things that you kept nodding at. One of the things he asked was whether you 'fancied his nephew'—did you know that?" Colin looked at Liv, hopeful. She shook her head, but a slow smile spread across her face. He continued, "I, ah, I didn't want to bring it up then—you know, Josh and all—but . . . well, is there any chance that could be true?"

Liv began to nod, then paused. She

wasn't sure where this conversation was going, but she needed to clear something up. "What about Lucy, the girl from the play? Aren't you together?"

"Me and Lucy? Hmm." Colin scratched his head. "Sure, we've been together about seventeen years." He broke into a huge smile. "Liv, Lucy is my little sister. She was in town visiting me from Stratford. She loves Shakespeare, so we decided to go to the show. She thought you were very nice, by the way. Josh Cameron—not so much."

"Oh," Liv said, suddenly completely at ease. "I see. So you're not . . . together, together."

"Not quite. Liv, I wanted to ask you out the first night I met you—but you were distracted with . . ." He gestured to Josh Cameron, who had begun to break-dance on the dance floor. "And then after our day in London, and the night at the Globe . . . but I just couldn't compete."

"Is it too late?" Liv wondered, not immediately realizing she'd said it aloud.

Colin shook his head and tiny little dimples popped up in his cheeks. He looked so adorable that Liv just couldn't stop herself. So she leaned her face toward his, and hoped that—for once—she wasn't saying or doing the wrong thing. As their lips touched, Liv could feel a smile tugging at the edges of Colin's mouth. She smiled back, thinking about how long it had taken to get it right.

As she relaxed into the kiss, Liv could have sworn she heard Anna and Francesco whooping from across the dance floor.

Dancing Queen

"Oh, Li-uhv, you look so pretty. Ah had no idea you could clean up so nicely." Rebecca smiled sweetly, then turned to address My Rover, who was sitting regally on a captain's chair in the corner of Music Mix's hair and makeup room. "Doesn't she just look adorable, baby? Yes, she does. Yesss sheee does!"

Liv rolled her eyes in the mirror. She understood after all that Rebecca really wasn't mean. She was just really, really weird. Colin was somehow able to find humor in her oddities, but Liv still had a way to go before she could actually be *entertained* by Rebecca. In the meantime, at least they were getting along.

Right after the Josh Cameron concert, Rebecca had quickly and happily agreed to help Anna and Liv with hair, makeup, and "style" for their VJ for a Day audition. And now, three weeks later, with just minutes before they were on, she was fluffing and puffing Liv's hair to perfection.

Anna was ready to go on, and was standing outside the soundstage door, running through her lines one last time before their session kicked off. Everything—the music, script, props, and costumes—was all set. Now it would just come down to the execution, and whether they could pull it off was still to be seen.

There were a total of five auditions, and Liv and Anna had been selected to go last. They had been waiting and prepping for several hours in a tiny room just down the hall from the *Hits Parade* studio as the other intern teams wrapped their sessions. Almost every intern had formed a team with others, and the competition had gotten intense in the past week as the day of taping drew nearer. Though the auditions weren't live— the winner's segment would air on Music Mix that afternoon—all the auditions were being taped without do-overs in the *Hits Parade* studio.

For their audition, Liv and Anna had decided to stage a series of Make Me a Star segments, in which several "regular" people would be made over to look, dress, and act like celebrities. The makeovers would be done in real time, interspersed with the day's top Video Hits.

If everything went as planned, viewers would see people go from Frumpy to Fabulous in just under an hour. Ideally, the "drama" of waiting for the final result would keep people tuned in throughout the show. The outlandish disco gear Anna had found in old Music Mix wardrobe closets guaranteed that the production would be a visual success, if nothing else.

Naturally, Liv and Anna had decided to use ABBA's "Dancing Queen" as the backdrop to their audition. The "regular" people would be morphed into the band ABBA and, at the end of the show, would do a silly dance performance as the band.

True to her word, Christy Trimble had answered Liv's call for help, and had eagerly agreed to help them with the final dance— she had won Best Pop Video at the VMAs the past two years, and was known to be an exceptional choreographer. But she had agreed to help under one condition: Christy thought it would be "fabulously funny" if Josh Cameron were one of the makeover victims. Liv had agreed, assuming Josh would *never* go for it—after all, he was far from "regular." But when Christy called Josh and told him that this would be a good way for him to make himself seem approachable and "down-to-earth," he quickly agreed.

Liv and Anna were the two female makeover victims. Anna would also be the main VJ, and Liv would handle all the behind-the-scenes, makeover-in-progress interviews. After much begging and pleading, Liv had finally managed to convince Colin to be the second guy in the band, rounding out their ensemble.

Now, with only a few seconds to go, Liv hoped Josh—or anyone else in the "band"— wouldn't flake out. As the two-minute warning bulb flashed, Liv scurried off in search of Anna. Showtime!

"I look like someone's dad," Josh Cameron surveyed himself in the mirror while rubbing his short, tan beard. "Are you sure about this beard?"

Liv stifled a laugh, while Rebecca reassured him he looked "mah-vel-ous." They were about half an hour into the audition, and the cameras were in Josh's dressing room to check in on his "Frumpy to Fabulous" makeover status. As Liv stood waiting for the cameras to roll (Video Hit #8 was just about to end), she chose not to tell Josh how he really looked. Rather than normal and approachable, as Christy had promised him, Liv sort of thought Josh seemed a little pitiful and desperate for doing this. But he was oblivious.

"You look fabulous," she said, just as the cameras flipped on. "Now—smile, Mr. Cameron!"

"Liv," Anna whispered. "My butt cheeks are showing. Any suggestions?" Liv glanced across the set, giggling uncontrollably as Anna spun around and wiggled her butt. She was right—her short, white dress left little to the imagination. But the effect was perfect.

Anna and Liv were wearing matching white retro dresses, both of which were tied around the waist with a gold belt. Anna's hair had been covered with a long blond wig, and Liv's naturally curly brown hair was puffed into an aerobic-instructor do. Both girls had a gold headband tied across their foreheads, and were wearing moccasin-style boots that laced up their legs. Liv had to admit it—Rebecca was a makeup genius and Anna had perfected her wardrobe skills. They really did make a great team.

Liv stole a quick glance at Colin, who turned and flashed a toothy smile. Liv burst out laughing. A few weeks ago she never could have imagined Colin would agree to do something like this, but now he was a natural. He had mastered the dance (which frightened her just a little), and had happily zipped himself into *the* ugliest white jumpsuit she had ever seen. Rebecca had outfitted him in a flowing brown wig and a sporty headband. He looked like the ultimate porn star.

Anna came up behind Liv to check out Colin's ridiculous getup. "He's your soul mate," she whispered to Liv, laughing. "A loveable dork—with absolutely no inhibitions. I never would have guessed."

Liv turned and squeezed Anna's hands. "This is it," she said. "Only one more chance to make complete fools of ourselves. You are totally rocking—if they don't offer you a job after this, they're crazy!"

"Gaaaah! Don't say that. You're freaking me out!" Anna said, grinning.

"We," Liv said, squeezing Anna into a

hug, "are going to rock. Now, as Brown would say . . . Go, Girl!" Then she pushed Anna out onto center stage as the producers signaled the end of Video Hit #2.

The lights splashed onto the stage, and Anna lifted the mic to her mouth and flashed a huge smile. "The moment we've been waiting for is finally here," she said into the camera, just as Francesco cued up "Dancing Queen" on the stereo in the background. "Today's top video?" she continued. "Nuh-uh—that will have to wait. First, the grand finale of our Make Me a Star makeovers. We've gone from frumpy . . . to fabulous! Ladies and gentlemen, please welcome . . . ABBA!"

The first notes of "Dancing Queen" came pouring out of the speakers as Anna ripped off the tracksuit she had thrown on to cover her outfit. Liv joined her in the center of the *Hits Parade* stage. Back-to-back, they held their microphones up and lip-synched in time to the music. *"You can dance, you can jive, having the time of your life . . ."*

As the second verse started, Colin and Josh popped out from opposite sides of the stage. Josh's outfit was exactly the same as Colin's, but instead of a wig, his naturally curly hair had been straightened into a helmetlike flop over his face. Liv could hear the producers and camera operators chuckling as Josh and Colin swayed out onto the stage. They moved and shook their hips in time to the music, fanning their hands out every time *"ooh ooh ooh"* came pouring out of the speakers.

At the end of the song, the foursome all slid to their knees, arms raised, and held their pose while Anna pointed to the camera and introduced Cherie Jacobson's new single as that day's top video. "I hope you've had as much fun as we have," she said, winking. "Live it up, Dancing Queens!"

One of the camera operators shouted, "That's a wrap!" Liv sighed a breath of relief. She and Anna cheered as Rebecca came running out from backstage. The three roommates danced around in a circle, hugging and laughing. *We did it,* Liv thought happily. *We actually did it.*

Later that afternoon everyone gathered at O'Leary's, an Irish pub around the corner from the Music Mix offices. The owner, a shrunken, stooped Irish fellow, had agreed to air that afternoon's *Hits Parade* segment on the bar's TV. Andrew Stone would be broadcasting the winner's segment as part of that day's show, and until the broadcast, they were left in suspense, waiting to see who won.

A few minutes before *Hits Parade* started, Simon Brown entered the bar and lazily made his way to an armchair in a corner of the room. Liv stole a glance at Anna, who had been working up the courage to talk to Brown all day. Anna's mom had called that morning, saying she could accept that her daughter needed to figure her life out—and together, they had resolved that if Anna got a job offer from Music Mix, she would stay in London for one more year before deciding her next step. Liv knew her roommate was making herself sick wondering whether things would work out. Liv crossed her fingers and glanced at Brown slumped in the corner.

Anna caught Liv's eye before slowly making her way across the room to where Brown was sitting alone with a cigarette and a beer (Liv could only assume he had a fat wad of Nicorette tucked in each cheek). Liv watched Anna approach him. Knowing Brown had the power to dramatically transform Anna's future, Liv considered the fact that she would need to figure out her own future pretty soon. Living in London had been the only thing she'd ever really *known* she wanted to do, and it had turned out to be a perfect choice.

Though Liv didn't know for sure what her next move would be, Anna had helped her realize that uncertainty could be okay. She just needed to think a lot more clearly and carefully about what she *might* want to do after graduation next year. She smiled at Colin, who had been watching her from across the bar. He moved over to her and pulled her in for a kiss.

"I can't believe you have to leave," he murmured in her ear. "Stay."

Liv wrapped her arms around Colin's neck. "Mmmm," she murmured as she snuggled into the crook of his neck and breathed in deeply—she loved that Colin smelled like a combination of fabric softener and soap. If she had known how comfortable that crook was, she definitely wouldn't have waited so long to get rid of Josh Cameron. She just wished she had more time to burrow into Colin's neck before she had to go back to the States.

"I really don't want to waste our time together thinking about me leaving," she said, leaning back and looking into his eyes. "And who knows what could happen?

Maybe I'll be back next summer. . . . My mom left London to come to the States—what's keeping me from taking her place in England?"

"You would really come back?" Colin said, brushing a stray curl off her face with his finger.

"This summer sort of proved that anything can happen, didn't it?" She leaned forward and brushed his lips with hers. He pulled her in tighter.

"I hate to interrupt." Anna had materialized at Liv's side, smiling broadly. Liv and Colin broke apart, and Liv looked at her roommate expectantly. Anna continued, "Guess who's staying in London?"

"You got a job?!" Liv asked, her excitement bubbling up.

Anna nodded. "Apparently, Gloria was just offered a position as a VJ—so her job is open." Anna was beaming. "Brown said it's mine if I want it! I guess my supervisor in wardrobe talked to him a few days ago and recommended me. Brown said he was impressed that I approached him—that it proves how much I want it."

Liv was ecstatic. She quickly gathered Anna into a huge hug, just as Francesco danced over. Colin and Francesco exchanged a shrug and then wrapped Anna and Liv into a big four-person hug. Liv broke away just in time to see the *Hits Parade* logo pop up onto the TV in the corner. The show was about to start.

She reached for Anna's hand, and they held their breath, waiting to see who had won. Liv closed her eyes—she couldn't stand the suspense. She reminded herself that even if they hadn't won, their performance—and Anna's job offer—had been a truly perfect ending to a perfect summer.

Just as the first notes of "Dancing Queen" came floating out of the television set, Rebecca's high-pitched yell cut through the din of the bar—"Ah did it!" she screamed, lifting My Rover into the air. "Li-uhv, Anna, I won!"

Some things never change. But for Liv and Anna, so much had.

And Liv was having the time of her life.

About the Author

Erin (Soderberg) Downing is a former children's book editor who now works at Nickelodeon. Her guilty pleasures include an unhealthy obsession with reality TV, an addiction to *Us Weekly*, and Magnolia Bakery cupcakes. A native of Duluth, Minnesota, Erin has lived in both England and Sweden and currently resides in New York City with her husband and newborn daughter.

I could keep my expressionless drum major face on while I strode under the bleachers and around the stadium to the bathroom. But then I was going to bawl.

Six thousand people, almost half the town, came to every home game of the high school football team. Tonight they crowded the stadium for the first game of the season. They had expected the band to be as good as usual. Instead, it had been the worst halftime show ever to shatter a hot September night. And I'd been in charge of it.

Me and the other drum major, Drew Morrow.

Allison knew exactly what I was doing. She handed her batons to another majorette and hurried close behind me.

The band always took third quarter off. So I had about half an hour to get myself together, with Allison's help, before I had to be back in the stands to direct the band playing the fight song during fourth quarter.

I felt Allison's hand on my back, supporting me, as I stepped through the bathroom door. My eyes watered, my nose tickled, I was ready to let loose—

Unfortunately, about twenty girls from the band were in the bathroom ahead of me. Including Drew's girlfriend of the month, the Evil Twin.

Allison stepped in front of me, putting herself between me and them. She seemed nine feet tall. She was a lot more threatening dressed in her majorette leotard than I was dressed like a boy. But she pulled at her earring with one hand, so I knew she was stressing out.

The Evil Twin was either Tracey or Cacey Reardon—I wasn't sure which one, and no one else seemed to know either. All we knew for sure was that the twins were evil. Or, one of them was evil and the other just looked the same.

I assumed the one currently dissing me was the one dating Drew. Because she sure seemed to have it in for me.

I pulled Allison toward the door. I could cry later.

Before we managed to leave, the twin

turned back to Allison and made the mistake of touching her majorette tiara.

Allison whirled around with her claws out.

"Fight!" someone squealed. Several freshmen made it out the door, still shrieking.

I hadn't witnessed a fight like this since a couple of girls got into it over a Ping-Pong game in seventh grade PE. And I was about to be the costar.

"Hey!" Drew boomed in his drum major command voice. His tall frame filled the doorway.

Allison and the twin stopped. There was complete silence for two seconds at the shock of getting caught. Then everyone realized it was Drew, not a teacher, and screamed because there was a boy in the girls' bathroom.

Drew reached through the girls. I thought he was reaching for the twin to save her from herself. But his hand closed over *my* wrist. I stumbled after him as he dragged me out of the bathroom and through the line at the concession stand, to a corner behind a concrete pillar that held up the stadium.

He let go of my wrist. "What. Were. You. *Doing?*"

I was gazing way up at the world's most

beautiful boy. Drew was a foot taller than me and had a golden tan, wavy black hair, and deep brown eyes fringed with dark, thick lashes. And these were almost the first words he'd spoken to me since the band voted us both drum majors last May.

"Your girlfriend started it. Why don't you talk to *her*?"

"My girlfriend isn't drum major."

"So?"

"So, it's bad enough that I have to be drum major with you. It's bad enough that the band sounded like crap tonight. But you are *not* going to get in fights with people in the band. We have the same position. If *you* stoop to that level, *I've* stooped to that level. I'm not going to let you make me look irresponsible."

I had already known this was the way he felt about me. He'd tried his best during summer band camp to act like I didn't exist. Except when he spoke low to the trombones and they muttered under their breath as I passed.

"You're not my boss." My voice rose. "You don't get to tell me what to do."

He leaned farther down toward me and hissed, "We are not going to yell at each other in public. Do you understand?"

"You are not going to get in my face and threaten me. Do *you* understand?"

"Good job, drum majors!" called some trumpets passing by. They gave us the thumbs-up and sarcastic smiles. "Teamwork— who needs it?"

Behind them, Allison waited for me against the wall, arms folded, tiara askew.

I turned my back on Drew. We weren't through with our discussion, but we weren't going to solve anything by trading insults. And I wanted to make sure all Allison's cubic zirconia were in place.

I was glad about the quasi-catfight. I was glad Drew had reprimanded me too. Now I was pissed with the band and with Drew, instead of mortified at myself for being such a bad drum major on my first try.

And it was nice to find out that Drew knew I existed, after all.

"I hate this town, I hate this town, I hate this town," Allison chanted for a few minutes after we sat down in the stands. I sent our friend Walter to fetch her makeup case from her car, knowing that makeup could distract her from anything. She would feel better when she was back to looking like her usual self.

Allison leaned closer and said quietly,

"You don't want him to know you're upset."

Then, like the dorks we were, we both turned around and looked at Drew, who sat with his dad at the top of the football stadium. Grouped on the rows between us and Drew, several trumpet players and saxophone players glared at me like they wanted to pitch me off the top railing. In fact, Drew and his dad probably would have been glad to help me over.

I felt a pang of jealousy. Drew was close to his dad. I could tell the conversation Drew and his dad were having at the moment wasn't pleasant, but at least they were having one. I hardly talked to my dad anymore.

"Foul!" Walter jeered at the game, startling me and making Allison jump on my other side.

Walter handed Allison her makeup case and looked at me. "I also put Drew's band shoes back in his truck, like we found them."

"Thanks." Drew made me mad playing Mr. Perfect all the time. I had thought it would make me feel better to hide his lovingly polished band shoes so he had to wear his Vans with his band uniform. It hadn't.

"So, what happened in the halftime show?" Walter asked. "It reminded me of the Alabama Symphony Orchestra, but not in a good way. You know, before they start playing together, when they're tuning up."

Allison nodded. "There's a point in the majorette routine when I'm supposed to throw the baton on one and turn on two. I looked up at Drew and thought, *Is he on one? No, two.* And then I looked over at you, and you were on, like, thirty-seven."

I just shook my head. I was afraid that if I tried to talk about it right now, the pissed feeling would fade, the mortified feeling would come back, and I'd start bawling in front of the tuba players.

Walter slid his arm around my waist, and Allison draped her arm around my shoulders from the other side. I tried to feel better, not just sweatier. They were the two best possible friends.

Someone slid onto the bench beside Walter. Oh no, Luther Washington or one of Drew's other smart-ass trombone friends coming to rub it in. Or worse, the Evil Twin. I peered around Walter.

It was the new band director, Mr. Rush.

Before I'd seen him today, I'd hoped that getting a new band director might help my predicament as queen band geek. Mr. O'Toole, who'd been band director for as long as I could remember, had gotten us into this mess by deciding we'd have two drum majors this year.

Then, knowing he'd be leaving near the beginning of the school year anyway, he sleepwalked through summer band camp. He let Drew and me avoid working together. I couldn't imagine what the new band director would be like, but any change had to be for the better.

Or not. Mr. Rush didn't seem like he was in any position to change the status quo. He was fresh out of college and looked it, maybe twenty-two years old. He could have passed for even younger, and I wondered how Mr. Rush thought he could handle a hundred and fifty students.

I was about to find out.

"Amscray," Mr. Rush growled at Walter. Walter leaped up and crossed behind me to sit on Allison's other side.

Mr. Rush stared at me. Not the stare you give someone when you're starting a serious conversation. Worse than this. A deep, dark stare, his eyes locking with mine.

He meant to intimidate me. He wanted me to look away. But I stared right back. It felt defiant, and I wondered whether I could get suspended for insubordination just for staring.

I guess I passed the test. Finally he relaxed and asked, "What's your name?"

"Virginia Sauter."

He nodded. "What's the other one's name?" He didn't specify "the other suck-o drum major," but I knew what he meant.

I shuddered. "Drew Morrow."

Walter leaned around Allison. "His friends call him General Patton."

Allison laughed.

Mr. Rush ignored them. He asked me, "What's with the punky look? You've got the only nose stud I've seen in this town."

"Would you believe she entered beauty pageants with me until two years ago?" Allison asked. Allison always rubbed this in.

"I developed an allergy to taffeta," I said.

"No, she didn't," Allison said. "On the first day of summer band camp in ninth grade, she walked by Drew in the trombone section. The trombones called her JonBenét Ramsey, and it was all over. She quit the majorettes and went back to drums."

"Is that true?" Walter asked me.

"You think I was born with a stud in my nose?"

"And she stopped wearing shoes," Allison added.

Mr. Rush eyed my band shoes.

"Well, I'm wearing shoes *now*," I said. "Of course I can't be out of uniform at a game."

"Of course not," Mr. Rush said, looking my uniform up and down with distaste.

"More people might get their noses pierced if I started a club," I said. "Would you like to be our faculty sponsor?"

"And an attitude to match the nose stud," Mr. Rush said. He leaned across me to point at Allison and Walter. "You, princess. And you, frog. Beat it."

They scattered, leaving Mr. Rush and me alone on the bench.

He glanced over his shoulder at Drew and his father at the top of the stands. "What's up with you and Morrow?"

"He was drum major by himself last year," I said. "Everybody knew he'd be drum major again this year. But Clayton Porridge was trying out against him. I wanted to be drum major next year, after Drew graduated. I figured I'd better go ahead and try out, just for show, so Clayton wouldn't have anything on me."

I looked down into my cup of ice. "I never thought I'd make it this year. A girl has never been drum major. And we've never had two drum majors. Mr. O'Toole decided after the vote that we'd have two this year, the two with the most votes, and that was Drew and me. I don't know what he was thinking." I made a face. "Though I'm pretty sure what Drew's thinking."

"So a girl's never been drum major," Mr. Rush repeated slowly. "And all the flutes and clarinets are girls, and all the trombones are boys. Gotta love a small town steeped in tradition. Who needs this diversity crap?"

It bothered me, too, or I wouldn't have tried out for drum major.

"Which one of you got the most votes?" he asked.

"Mr. O'Toole wouldn't tell us."

Allison had a theory, though. She thought I won, and Mr. O'Toole just didn't want me to be drum major by myself. I mean, he didn't even want to let a girl try out. My dad had to threaten to call the school board.

I went on, "Mr. O'Toole said that since we were both drum majors, it didn't matter who got more votes. He didn't want to generate bad blood between us." I smiled and said sarcastically, "It.worked."

Mr. Rush rubbed his temple like he had a headache. "When's the last time you had a conversation with Morrow?"

"A conversation?"

"Yeah, you know. You talk, he talks, you communicate."

"We had an argument just now because he sicced his girlfriend on me in the bathroom. Is that progress?"

He closed his eyes and rubbed his temple harder. "How about before that?"

"Communicate. Probably . . ." I had to think about this. "Never."

"Then how have you functioned at all? Even on your sad, limited level?"

I shrugged. "Mr. O'Toole would tell me where to go on the field, and then he would tell Drew where to go."

Mr. Rush muttered, "You see me in my office before band practice when we come back to school on Tuesday. And I want you to spend the long weekend contemplating how the two of you reek."

"I know," I whispered.

"If you performed that way at a contest, you'd get embarrassingly low marks. So would the band, because the two of you have them so confused. And the drums! Though I'm not sure the drums are your fault. I suspect they reek on their own merit."

He stood, looking down at me with a diabolical grin. "I'm so glad we've had this chat. To be fair, I'd give Morrow the same treatment, but it looks like someone's beat me to it."

I nodded. "His father and his two older brothers used to be drum majors."

"What? A legacy? The Morrow clan has drum major tied up like the Mafia?"

"It feels that way."

"I should have kept my job in Birmingham at Pizza Hut," Mr. Rush grumbled as he stomped away down the bleachers.

I had to agree with this. Despite myself, I looked up one more time at Drew high in the stands. He and his father sat side by side in the same position, leaning forward, elbows on knees. The only difference was that Drew hung his head. Now Mr. Morrow pointed to Drew's Vans.

I imagined Mr. Morrow lecturing Drew in a Tony Soprano voice. "I'm counting on you to uphold the family name. I want you to off the broad. *Capisce?*"